BLOODY BIZARRE

Short Stories

By Andy Day

Anything you set your mind to	4
The Universe hates you	7
Pete's Garden	10
One bad day	15
Tubbies	20
The Interrupter	23
The VHS Premonition	26
VR	32
Big Bad	37
Naughty or nice	39
Ronald's Garden	45
The Prisoner	46
The Cursed Stones	54
Wake, work, sleep, repeat.	65
The ugly duckling	67
The Pervy Fly	75
The Lying Fly	77
Number 18	80
Rover	82
Future Theatre	84
How are you?	89
First time, last time	91
What's your name again?	93

Role Play	98
The Superhero	103
The Superhero ii	109
What makes a hipster?	110
When in Rome	115
Assassin	116
Nihilist	124
The itch	126
Infinite Monkeys	128
Want to live forever?	131
Diarrhoea	132
The Island of Peace and Love	138
Fairies	145
Crush	149
The Superhero iii	151
Rolos	153
Flight F7401	161
You know that dream	166
Beard Theory	168
Worst DJ ever	171
The Cremation of Charlie Hutchins	175
Jurassic Show And Tell	185
Cupid's Arrow	187

Anything you set your mind to

1

....

Joe was born on 21 August 1947 at the home of his parents, John and Grace Hubert. Grace gave birth so suddenly that she didn't have time to get to the hospital. The birth wasn't the kind you saw on tv — it had more of a burst carrier bag vibe — but instead of vegetables, eggs, and milk falling out of the bottom, it was a baby followed by what could be mistaken for offal and red wine. And shit. It wasn't a typical food shop. She always joked that Joe had no patience, 'You've always been the same; couldn't even wait to get out of my uterus' she would say, scolding him throughout his childhood for his lack of self-control. But she took comfort in the fact that this trait also contributed to his high-ambitions — as Joe was never willing to wait for the next opportunity — he would always create it.

Throughout School, Joe succeeded in his academic studies and sports alike. He got on to the school football team by taking the place of another schoolboy, Peter, who'd mysteriously come down with severe diarrhoea — but as I said, Joe created his own opportunities — on this occasion, by taking advantage of his Uncle's pharmacy — a drug treasure trove he had full access to whilst minding the place when his uncle popped out for a cigarette. Joe helped himself to as many laxatives as he could cram into his pockets. Peter shat his pants at school and was off for two weeks - mainly due to the shame and embarrassment, and only partly due to his explosive diarrhoea, which only lasted forty-eight hours.

Joe was a natural at sports - not as great as Peter but nonetheless impressive. He wasn't career-worthy talented, but talented enough to be impressive amongst a mishmash of reprobates the school inaccurately described as athletes.

Joe's attention span in class was poor. His teachers, knowing his exam results were exemplary, could only assume that the classes just didn't challenge his keen mind. They accepted that he'd get the results he wanted and therefore weren't too concerned whether or not he paid any attention in class. You see, Joe was a dreamer - he stared out of the classroom window across the football field and cast his mind far, far away.

'Mum! Dad!' Joe bellowed at the top of his pre-pubescent underdeveloped lungs. 'I want to be a footballer when I'm older.' His Dad gave a little smile from behind his broadsheet, and his mother responded dismissively, 'Never mind football', and smacked the back of his head and told him to go wash his hands before dinner.

A year later, Joe had come home from school with a glowing report card. His teachers wanted to highlight Joe's exam results and sporting achievements. 'Mum! Dad! I want to be a doctor when I grow up!' Joe said with a precocious resolve. This time, instead of dismissing his ambition and clouting him across the back of his head, Grace Hubert, clutching her son's report card, looked down at Joe with a maternal pride in her expression he'd not witnessed before. His mother simply said, 'You can do anything you set your mind to'.

Another year passed, and Joe came home and announced his latest dream. 'I want to be an actor' he said, with the same certainty and resolve he'd expressed the previous two times he'd found his calling. 'You can be anything you want to be, love' replied his mother. His father piped up, 'We've always said it lad, you can do anything you set your mind to'.

Another year passed. Joe came home, covered in acne and smelling like a sweaty teenager in cheap cologne — which of course, he was. 'Mum, Dad - I really think I've found my career now! I'm going to focus on writing - I think I'll be a great journalist or novelist'.

'You can do anything you set your mind to petal' said his mother nonchalantly, her eyes not moving a nanometre from her knitting.

Years passed yet again, and Joe had finished school and was working part-time at his local DIY store. Joe wasn't a genius after all. He'd been cheating on just about every exam he'd ever taken. What was real however, was his ambition and drive.

He'd decided to take a gap year before applying to do something at college. Joe had no idea what he actually wanted to do with his life. He'd changed his mind so many times that he'd forgotten his previous career goals. Months passed, and he finally decided, *I want to be an artist.* Joe decided to go to art school and learn his trade. He wanted to be well-respected, well-paid, held in high-esteem by his peers, and praised by the critics. After all, *he could be anything he wanted to be; do anything he set his mind to!*

On 21st August 2020, Joe turned 73. He had a heart-attack stacking a shelf at the DIY shop he'd never left. It was his birthday, and his final thought before shuffling off this mortal coil was that his parents were lying bastards, and bad parents.

Don't believe your parents, kids - your life will be just as meaningless and disappointing as theirs.

2

Jamal had a belief. He believed that someone or something would not allow him to be happy. He believed someone or something, whether it be God, or a conscious universe, would actively act as a hindrance in his life. Maybe they got a perverse kick out of his suffering.

Jamal's life had been an uphill struggle from the very beginning. He received very little attention in his first few months of life, as his mother had suffered terribly with post-natal depression, and his father had no interest in being involved in childcare. As he grew older, his teachers recognised his learning difficulties. Jamal had to work so much harder than everyone else just to keep up.

Jamal was bullied. School was torture — a prison. Actual prisoners were imprisoned for a crime - they knew why they were there — Jamal couldn't work out what he'd done to deserve the same kind of treatment. He had no choice but to be condemned to his own personal Hell.

After school, he'd rush home as soon as the bell rang, hoping to avoid the other kids walking home. But his home-life wasn't much better and he couldn't wait to escape.

Jamal wanted to be a singer — but he couldn't sing. He then wanted to be an actor — but he suffered terribly with his nerves and failed miserably when he tried auditioning. He ended up in a dead-end job working in an office as a data entry clerk.

Jamal's adult life was tedious to him. He lived in a tiny bedsit and couldn't afford much of a social life. He couldn't afford a mortgage or a car, or any extravagances.

Jamal had fallen in love a few times, but it was always one-sided. The feelings were never reciprocated and he'd never had a relationship - the universe wouldn't allow it. Every time he met someone he liked and wished to be with, it ended in his embarrassment following rejection.

Jamal decided he'd be content with companionship of any kind. He wanted a cat or a dog, but he was allergic, plus his landlord wouldn't allow pets. He only wanted companionship, and not only wouldn't the universe allow him human companionship, it wouldn't even allow him companionship from a bloody animal either. He couldn't even get a cat! Unbelievable! Jamal was convinced someone was taking the piss.

His hair fell out prematurely, and he suffered with innumerable ailments.

Jamal hadn't achieved anything in life and he was bitter.

One day, Jamal met a Genie. He made a wish. He wasn't allowed three wishes, as was the common misconception, but allowed only one. Jamal thought for one moment, then made his wish. He wished for a cat without an allergy.

Jamal was to be evicted from his flat for breaching the terms of his lease agreement. On moving day, he awoke in his bed to find his affectionate cat sat on his chest, pawing at his pyjama shirt.

Jamal smiled. The cat leaned forward and licked Jamal's face. His airways tightened and anaphylaxis killed him within minutes. He'd phrased his wish badly. The cat he'd wished for didn't have any allergies. Jamal however, retained his. The Genie smiled a sinister smile and disappeared.

The universe laughed so hard, it wet itself — before moving on and choosing someone else to torment.

And then it chose you. Soz.

Pete's Garden

3

Pete didn't know how he'd ended up lying naked in his garden staring up at the scorching sun, but he knew it was probably best he get indoors before his tanned skin turned into burnt skin. He was covered in dirt, so that must have given him some protection, thought Pete.

He'd never noticed the wheelbarrow before — it was a very large wheelbarrow and Pete wondered how it had made its way into his garden. There was something sinister and foreboding about that wheelbarrow, and Pete didn't much enjoy the anxiety he was now feeling. He averted his stare and decided to head indoors immediately.

Unfortunately, Pete couldn't move. 'What is happening?' Pete panicked 'I can't move! I can't move!'. His mind was racing and he screamed out in anguish! Except, he couldn't vocalise his anguish — the screaming was all in his mind. He was paralysed. *Maybe I've been attacked and left for dead! I don't remember anything!*

After some time passed, Pete's anguish and internal cries faded away into the dreamworld. He was exhausted. Pete had fallen asleep in his garden yet again.

Pete didn't know he was dreaming; as far as he was concerned, he really was playfully rolling down a grassy hill like a child, until the decline levelled off, slowing him down until he reached a standstill before wobbling to a halt. His eyes hurt from the brightness of the sun, and for reasons unbeknownst to Pete, his skin began to turn green. He despaired over his transformation and his dream turned into a nightmare. A giant border collie dog ran over to him and bit him hard. The pain shot across his body and shocked Pete awake — and he found himself once again, lying naked in his garden. Pete was thankful there was no giant dog and relieved his skin hadn't turned green.

However, Pete *was* in pain. His sides felt like they'd been pierced just like in his dream. Had the pain he'd felt in his dream been transferred to his subconscious from an external stimulus? Had he been hurt in the real-world? Had someone or something attacked him?

Pete still couldn't move — adding to the agony that lingered and followed him from the dog bite nightmare. How he longed for the beautiful bright green grassy hill he'd blissfully rolled down just minutes earlier — even if it wasn't real — it was better than this. Better than paralysis! As his mind frantically sifted its way through all of the hypothetically fatal scenarios it could conceive, such as hypothermia, starvation, dehydration, or even a dog attack, Pete saw something glistening in the sunlight, about a foot and a half away from him, lying on the grass. It had a dark green plastic triangular handle that merged into the wooden shaft, which merged with a metal socket, which quadfurcated into four shiny tines. It was a fork. A gardening fork. Is this what someone had used to attack him? Had the attacker now fled?

Pete lay helpless - wondering when someone would come to his aid, yet feeling somewhat calmer than before. He'd accepted he couldn't move and needed help - and it would surely come soon. He had hope.

Pete's attention was drawn to the sound of heavy boots on dry grass. Each boot thumped as it landed, sending reverberations through the ground which Pete felt beneath him. *Help! Help me please - I can't move and I think I've been attacked! Hello? Are you there?* Pete realised his words were only an internal monologue - they did not manifest as audible words. There was no response. Pete tried desperately to roll onto his side so he could see who was approaching - but his efforts were in vain. The boots grew closer and Pete's fear turned to panic, it had dawned on him that the attacker might have returned. *Please - take what you want - but please don't hurt me. I can't move. I think I'm badly hurt. Please, just leave me alone! Please?* But his words were yet again trapped inside his head. *Why couldn't he speak?* Pete begged as if his life depended on it. But the boots had stopped and there came no response. *Hello? Who's there? Show yourself damn you!*

Into Pete's field of view, came the bearded face of a weathered, wrinkly, but burly man. His broad shoulders, square jaw, and giant red ears made Pete feel tiny compared to this strapping beast of a man. The beastly man leaned over Pete in his dungarees and flat cap, scratched his head and with a confused expression on his face, reached down and seized Pete with his dirty bare-hands. Pete tried to struggle free but this bear of a man was too strong! *Get off me! What do you want? Please - please? I won't say anything if you let me go - I didn't see your face properly — this didn't happen! I won't tell - I won't tell! Please I'll do anything! Please!* Pete begged and cried like a terrified child, but to no avail. The brutish man paid Pete no heed - how could he, Pete couldn't make a sound. The coldness from the fiendish man sent shivers through Pete's very soul. He was drowning in his own fear and struggled to come up for air.

The beastly man flung Pete into the dreaded wheelbarrow. He knew he didn't like that wheelbarrow. Pete wasn't alone — he'd been thrown on top of others who'd met the same fate! *Why was this sick, twisted, evil bastard doing this? Who were the others? Were they still alive?* Pete tried to whisper to those beneath him but he still couldn't speak or move, and the others looked paralysed too.

At least Pete was still alive — maybe there was still a chance he'd be saved. He was being taken to the house and a woman in a floral apron and wearing hair curlers, opened the door. This was Pete's chance — she would see him in the wheelbarrow and surely contact the authorities. But it wasn't to be. *She has a smile on her face even though I'm clearly being abducted by this man — what is this twisted bitch up to? They're in it together, like Myra Hindley and Ian Brady!*

'You forgot a few dear — luckily I found them — can't have any getting away,' shouted the man with a jovial tone that deepened Pete's dreadful terror.

'Oh love — come out'tut'road - I'm about to start dinner — get a move on — and don't go dredging mud onto my clean kitchen floor - I've only just mopped it,' came the stern but playful reply. The cold casualness Pete had witnessed from the pair during such horrific and terrifying circumstances pushed him deeper into despair. Is this how his life would end? Would anybody remember him in years to come?

Pete had been taken by the man's partner-in-crime and was slumped over the kitchen table. The woman leaned in and frowned. At last - she's showing some emotion, thought Pete. The woman sighed, before holding up a small handheld instrument - it had sharp cerated metallic edges and Pete didn't like the look of it one bit. Over the next few seconds, Pete experienced a kind of agony he'd never thought possible. Excruciating cutting and stinging and burning pain, all rolled into one hellish torture. Pete was being flayed alive, and never before had flaying been carried out with such indifference and callousness - even during the worst times in history, flaying evoked some emotion, whether it be sickening disgust, or conversely, twisted delight. But never indifference. *Nobody before had ever whistled whilst skinning someone alive. Had they?* Pete must have passed out because he woke again to find himself lying in a row next to the other victims. He couldn't believe this was happening. He felt bad for a second as he'd had a wicked thought; he'd wished the twisted twosome would take the others but let him go.

Suddenly, the woman loomed over Pete and held aloft a very large, broad knife like a tennis player about to serve. She gripped the knife handle tightly, and swung the blade in a downwards motion, cutting Pete as easily as it had cut through the air. Pete was stabbed and cut and sliced again and again. The woman cut bits off him and sadistically left them lying next to him. Pete knew this was the end. There was no coming back from this.

Finally, his body, or what was left of it, was dangled over a vat of boiling water. Where did they obtain such a monstrous thing? Who owns a vat? This was it - Pete, in his final moments, writhing in the agony of being skinned alive, stabbed, sliced, and cut repeatedly, whispered his final prayers and, resigned to his horrific fate, waited for his excruciating end. As Pete was lowered into the boiling water, he wondered if anybody would remember him, or if anybody would care.

The answer was no. Because Pete was a potato, an actual potato. Not a couch-potato, but an actual potato.

Pete was delicious.

One bad day

4

Jonas overslept. He was always oversleeping, but this time he'd outdone himself. He was already an hour late when he woke up and shouted 'Fuck!'. He didn't have time for much as he had a meeting lined up for 10:30 a.m. He'd definitely be late for the meeting but the clients wouldn't be too offended by a ten minute delay - they could hob-knob over hob-knobs for a while. What could Jonas remove from his morning routine? Jonas settled on skipping his shower — he'd just keep his jacket on to contain the body odour and hope nobody noticed.

When Jonas got to the tube station, the announcement of severe delays on all underground lines came across the speaker system loud and clear. It felt like a personal insult and Jonas cursed Transport for London. Twenty minutes later, the tube arrived — it was jam-packed. He tried to squeeze on but people pushed past him and someone's elbow jabbed him in the ribs. 'Stand clear of the closing doors' said the pre-recorded voice. Jonas made one more attempt to squeeze on, but was shoved backwards by a labourer covered in presumably dried plaster, snapping 'I don't think so mate'. Jonas watched 3 more tubes come and go before he was able to finally board a carriage. He was now hot, sweaty and very annoyed.

On the carriage there were no seats, just elbows in his ribs, and armpits in his face. When it came to his stop, nobody made any concession to step aside and clear of the opening doors to let him off. He had to squeeze between the narrow gaps between inconsiderate commuters, 'excuse me. Excuse me please. Just fucking move you inconsiderate cunts', Jonas muttered under his breath.

Jonas was now much later than he'd intended. It was now 10:45 a.m. and he still had a ten minute walk to the office. The clients wouldn't be happy and the business relationship was already on thin ice. Leaving the station, Jonas realised he'd forgotten his case notes. 'Fuck!'.

He was nudged and shoulder barged a total of six times over the course of his commute. The slightest thing bumped his anger up another level. A man walked alongside him at a faster pace, who then decided he needed to spit on the floor. The breeze blew downwind and a few speckles of the slimy bodily projectile rode the wind and made their way into his face. 'What the fuck?' exclaimed Jonas. The man turned around, 'What?'.

'You dirty bastard — you spat in my face!' Jonas' arms were wide apart like Vitruvian man.

'Whatever,' replied the man, who continued to walk off at a faster pace. Jonas pulled out antibiotic wipes which he carried everywhere, and wiped his face. He used the whole packet, feeling disgusting and violated.

The office was within sight. He waited to cross the road — but there was no break in traffic and no pedestrian crossing — which always baffled and annoyed Jonas - who always told himself he'd write to the council about it, but never did.

Finally, a break in the traffic. He'd reached the office. Obviously, a pigeon shat on him first. Of course it did. Apparently it's lucky to be shat on by a bird, which Jonas thought was the most ludicrous concept ever imagined. It was like saying 'it's lucky to be hit by a bus' or 'it's lucky to be punched in the face'. Maybe an extreme exaggeration but Jonas didn't think so. He reached for his wipes, but realised he'd used them all wiping away a stranger's phlegm from his face, as you do.

Jonas got into the office - drowning in his own sweat and pigeon shit sliding down his face. He stormed into the office and apologised to his boss profusely. At least he had the sweat and shit on his face to prove how tragic his journey was. Maybe the clients would forgive him and the boss show leniency.

'Jesus - what happened to you' his boss enquired with genuine concern.

'Don't ask. Let me freshen up and I'll see the clients' replied Jonas.

'The clients? The clients are tomorrow' said the boss sympathetically, knowing this news was not what Jonas needed right now. 'You're on annual leave today - you booked it off months ago - you said you had an a-'

'Appointment' interrupted Jonas, his memory ignited.

Jonas was deflated. It was like he was a beanbag, and a fat St Bernard had just sat on him. He thought about it for a second. He pulled up his calendar on his phone:

"21.01.16 - 09:30 a.m. - Appointment - Clinic at Queen's Hospital - Memory Clinic"

'Fuck!'

Ironically, the appointment was for a memory clinic he'd been referred to by his GP. Jonas had epilepsy which affected his memory and the clinic needed epileptics with memory problems for a clinical trial. But he'd missed the appointment. This bad day wasn't good for his depression and anxiety. But maybe this is how the memory clinic got their data? They'd look at appointments scheduled against actual attendance, put it into a spreadsheet and Bob's your Uncle, useful statistical data and graphs and shit. Does anybody ever remember their appointments for memory clinic?

Jonas left the office and made the return journey home.

Jonas also threw himself onto the tracks that day.

The driver of the tube managed to slow down enough to save Jonas' life. It hit him at a near-fatal speed. Jonas spent the rest of his days being fed through a tube, unable to walk, and drooling like a St Bernard on a hot day. The 21.01.16 wasn't Jonas' day. Unlucky sod.

The driver of the tube never fully recovered psychologically and lost his job. His wife left him, unable to cope anymore, taking their children with her. The 21.01.16 wasn't his day either. A number of people were late because of the tube delays that day, all due to the incident on the tracks (or Jonas on the tracks to be more precise). One of them was on her way to visit her Son in the hospital who was in end stage renal failure. She'd only nipped home to collect some of his favourite toys he'd asked for, along with a new X-Men comic he wanted. She never made it back to the hospital in time to see her son go. Maybe he didn't want her to see him go, but as a result she never fully mentally recovered from the death of her son, and missing his final moment was too much to bear, and it was that guilty burden that took its toll and ended her life prematurely. She took a cocktail of pills and drifted away.

The knock-on-effect continued to ruin people's lives throughout the entire world. Jonas' bad day resulted in detrimental changes in the lives of millions. It also resulted in the election of

Donald Trump as President of the USA, Brexit, and the rise of Boris Johnson.

Damn commuters, damn pigeons. Damn memory clinic. Fucking butterfly effect.

ps. Does anybody ever make it to memory clinic? Or have I asked that already?

Tubbies

5

A long time ago on a far away planet, there lived 4 beings. These beings were the last of their kind and were technologically augmented with cranial antennae used for receiving signals from far away worlds, and view-screens housed in their distended abdomens for relaying signals to their kin. Each being had their own beautiful colour and uniquely shaped antenna.

For millennia, these beings played like children — their emotional development stunted due to the annihilation of their civilisation, along with any education or intelligent social interaction that once existed. They only had each other and the signals from far away worlds to learn from — which were mainly incoherent and incomprehensible.

Their home-world defied logic and reason. The beings' lives were overseen by a warm, bright & yellow creepy decapitated baby head in the sky that cruelly laughed at them each and every day, but brought them daylight too. The beings didn't know what this sinister infant sky-demon wanted — but they knew not to anger it. They only had a vague memory of those who came before, but the beings did remember one thing — one memory, one terrible, terrible memory. It was of their parents being flayed alive and set on fire by the giant baby head in the sky for failing to amuse it. Since then, the beings danced around and made silly noises to amuse the giant baby head - succumbing to its every whim in the fear of being punished.

Nobody knew what became of their civilisation - whether the baby head had wiped them all out or they'd somehow left of their own accord. Maybe the baby head was a being of such immense power and sadistic malevolence - that it got a sick thrill out of tormenting lesser beings and so the entire population had fled.

Thousands of years passed, and the colourful beings' delight in childlike pleasures had long-since died. Now, in their fully developed bodies, they desired greater stimulation. Their desires turned to grown-up things.

One of the beings learned to hone in on signals that introduced them to what you and I refer to as pornography; porn from hundreds of different alien civilisations. It seemed all alien races had porn in common.

This being, once a bright scarlet, was now a deeply faded red, with grey hair hanging like wilting plants from each ear and an antenna not as solid or tall as it once was. This being was abused horribly by the others - who used him for their deviant urges. The things they watched on his swollen belly - and the things they did on his swollen belly, and the things they left on..well, you get the picture, were degrading and humiliating. Until one day - the little red being stood before the omnipotent baby head in the sky and mooned it. Red was incinerated in a flash of blinding light. The baby head frowned.

The other three beings turned to a household appliance for their sexual gratification. The poor vacuum cleaner, cruelly designed with artificial intelligence, was used improperly day in, day out. Eventually, the machine had had enough; unable to live any longer being subjected to the unrelenting depravity, it self-destructed, killing the purple being, who'd been caught in the blast-radius. Purple had been particularly cruel to the little hoover — and the explosion had been timed perfectly.

Only two of the beings remained. They were bored, and depression kicked in. They were not as skilled as red had been at receiving signals from afar. But they had good memories and re-enacted the sordid scenes they remembered. Green's antenna proved extremely useful in their pursuit of sexual gratification, and yellow was pleased that he could use Green's phallic cranial appendage for his intimate needs, rather than for just receiving episodes of Newsnight and re-runs of Dallas.

Eventually, even this became boring, and the remaining two beings, Green and Yellow, needed greater stimulation. Their desires grew darker and darker. Yellow was strangling Green one evening, which they were both into, and something went wrong. Green had forgotten the safe word and Yellow continued to squeeze the life out of Green until they'd both reached climax and Green stopped breathing. "Uh Oh" cried Yellow.

Years passed with Yellow all alone. Food was running out and he'd already eaten the corpses of two of his deceased friends. No matter how hungry Yellow got, he refused to eat Green - he still liked to use the body for other things, from time to time.

Finally, Yellow passed away, alone and unhappy. He thought about the things he'd done — the depths of depravity he'd sunken to and how he'd do it all again if he could.

The decapitated baby head had dozed off after his execution of Red, and awoke to find his subjects gone. Angered by this - baby head left the planet burning in space - there would be no signs that life ever existed there. Baby head needed a new species to subjugate and torture, and the mood it was in, the next planet would be in for one hell of a global catastrophe. The suffering was going to be immeasurable. The baby head smiled, before blasting forward to its new destination - earth.

That was a few years ago. Should be here any time now.

The Interrupter

6

. . . .

There was something about Julie that everybody liked. She was kind and compassionate, strong-willed, determined, and reasonably intelligent — with a ditzy side most people recognised as deliberate.

Oliver was of the same camp as most — he thought Julie was nice enough — smiley, confident, good at her job — but there was one difference: there was something about Julie that he really, really didn't fucking like one bit.

One day, Oliver was in the office gathered around the water dispenser with a co-worker, James, when Julie popped over. Oliver and James were talking about their university experiences, way back when. Julie had arrived half-way through and quickly caught the gist of the conversation, and joined in. Julie joined in when Julie wanted to join in. She didn't have time for politeness, etiquette or other people's feelings, she had to say what she had to say, for what she had to say was more important or more interesting. Except that it wasn't.

'This is it!' thought Oliver. 'This is the thing that I don't like. This is why I hate Julie!'

Julie was an interrupter. What they have to say trumps what you have to say. You must have met these kinds of people yourself? Are they even listening to you? The answer is, they're not listening particularly, no.

The interruptions continued - day after day after day, until one day, Oliver thought, *No more!*

Oliver was talking with Thomas about his weekend in London. He'd travelled via two trains and was having a bit of a moan about ticket prices. His train ticket had cost him 60 quid one way. Outrageous. He then started talking about the show he'd caught in the West End. He'd been to see The Book of Mormon and loved it. He didn't notice Julie appear, but suddenly, just as he was talking about his favourite song in the show, and how funny it was, Julie started talking about the time she'd been to see Wicked in the West End.

Oliver continued to talk, he refused to stop just because Julie had joined in prematurely. He thought maybe she'd notice he was continuing to talk and realise he'd not finished, and maybe think to herself, *oh, how rude of me, Oliver hasn't finished.* But no. Julie continued to talk over him — she'd actually started talking slightly louder. *The fucking nerve!*

As the two spoke simultaneously - Thomas struggled to follow both dialogues and began to look a little uncomfortable. Oliver decided to start talking louder too, and eventually, the pair were shouting — not at each other, but at Thomas.

Finally, Oliver stopped and Julie continued. He shuffled between Julie and Thomas - turned his back to Julie, and continued his conversation. Julie continued to talk. Her commitment was unwavering. Thomas looked at Oliver and whispered, 'What is happening?'. Oliver explained, with Julie still waffling on about Wicked behind him, that she was extremely rude and always did this. Then he just snapped. He turned to Julie and shouted 'Oh will you just fuck off Julie, you ignorant cunt'. Silence. The whole office paused. All eyes were on Oliver. Julie was speechless.

'Finally,' said Oliver. 'So, there's this bit in Book of Mormon where they sing a song that sounds like something from the Lion King but it actually means..' Oliver spoke about The Book of

Mormon to the whole office, who were still stunned and thought maybe Oliver was having a breakdown. Either way, everyone had heard him lose his shit and verbally abuse Julie.

Later that day, Oliver cleared his desk and was escorted off the premises, *Totally worth it,* thought Oliver as he walked through the revolving doors of his office building holding a small cardboard box of his belongings.

As he stood outside the office, he took one last look up at the building and sighed. As he walked along adjacent to the building, he passed a window that was slightly open, and heard the words, 'Fuck you Julie you cunt'. Oliver smiled. One by one, the whole office would eventually experience Julie's rude behaviour.

Eventually, there were no employees left — they'd all told Julie to fuck off and had summarily been dismissed. Even the managers in charge and Human Resources had resigned, as there was no longer anyone left to manage other than Julie. The company could no longer function and inevitably collapsed. Julie had brought down a multi-million pound company, through interruption alone.

When Julie left the office for the final time; the last employee to leave, her phone rang and she answered promptly, speaking in a very serious tone, 'It's done. Awaiting my next assignment Sir'

Julie was - THE INTERRUPTER! Elite Corporate saboteur.

And still at large.

Is your company safe?

The VHS Premonition

7

There once was a magical place called Blockbuster video. This was a very long time ago when people were allowed out, and there was no such thing as Fortnight, Call of Duty, Netflix, or Covid-19. It was a simpler time. Nobody knew what a hashtag was. It was there but it was never used. It was simply waiting patiently for the future to arrive, where it would be needed. #JustSaying

Arnold was quiet and cold that night. Arnold was a town, not a person. In Arnold there was only two things to do on a Friday night — go to the local pubs, where drinking and fighting were the social norm, or there was Blockbuster; a wondrous place full of adventure, action, suspense, romance, thrills, comedy, horror, and science fiction. Tom and Stuart decided against a violent night out in Arnold, as most people had, judging by how quiet it was, and instead decided on renting a movie (or film, as it was known back then) in the form of a VHS tape. A VHS tape would be put into a VCR and connected to a TV the size of an oven. Not flat screen TV — no, these TVs were big fucking blocks. It's all very analogue and beyond your understanding.

Tom and Stuart wandered up and down separate aisles, browsing the videos from genre to genre, before convening at the *NEW RELEASES!* section. They'd decided to rent one new release, providing a copy was available, and one classic. That was their night sorted. Stuart had decided the classic should be A Nightmare on Elm Street. 'When I said classic, I meant like, Gone with the Wind, or Casablanca', said Tom, unimpressed with Stuart's choice. 'Come on! This is a classic! Fuckin' love this film mate', came an emphatic defence. Stuart loved horror films. Tom didn't - but didn't want to appear a wimp in front of his mate. So Freddy

Krueger it was. Now for the latest release; Tom was adamant he should have the final say on this. 'Whatever man - I've got what I came for', a nonchalant Stuart replied.

Pulp Fiction was the choice. Both friends seemed happy with their choices. They'd got to the counter, picked out some popcorn and sweets, and Tom proudly pulled out his Blockbuster membership card. The spotty teenager behind the counter took the card and typed the membership number into his computer — told Tom he had a late-return fine on his account, then scanned the film cases, popcorn and sweets with his barcode scanner. 'That'll be £14.98 please'. They pooled their funds, paid the spotty teen, and headed home to Tom's place.

Once home, the TV was switched on, the junk-food opened, and in slid the VHS into his JVC VCR. You may need to google these terms. Side note; Google wasn't around back then.

It was decided, by Stuart, that *his* film should be shown first. The Film started and both tensed up as they waited anxiously for the first Freddy scare.

The scenes were gruesome. Stuart smiled ear to ear like a complete weirdo, whilst Tom cringed and was more disturbed by Stuart's gratification from the horrific death scenes, than he was by Freddy Krueger.

As the film ended and the credits started, Stuart leant down to pick up some popcorn he'd clumsily dropped during the film — and ate them off the carpet, one by one — *waste not want not*. Suddenly, the rolling credits disappeared from the television screen, and a new scene appeared. 'Ooh what's this?' Tom asked excitedly. Stuart was still hunting for popcorn and barely registered Tom's enquiry. The scene was only a few seconds long. A guy, probably in his late 20s or early 30s is crossing a road, when out of nowhere another man in a red hoody barges into him, standing closely face to face, looks him straight in the eyes, grabs the back of his head with his left hand to draw him in close, then repeatedly stabs him until he falls to the ground, oozing with blood. The screen goes back to the credits. Stuart finally registers Tom's question and replies, 'What's what?'.

'What's what? What's what! What the fuck was that? That scene! Where's the remote? Have you got the remote? Rewind it — fucking rewind it!' Tom was clearly distressed.

'It's right there next to you. Jesus! What the fuck is wrong with you?' Stuart frowned at Tom.

'That scene! Stabbed - stabbed and blood everywhere!' Tom began mumbling and speaking gibberish - Stuart could only make out some of the words — like '*blood*' and '*knife*' and '*It's me*'.

'What scene? There were quite a few death scenes' Stuart let out a smug laugh.

As Tom frantically rewound the tape, then played, and rewound again, then fast-forwarded, then rewound - he rambled again, 'where is it? Where is it?'.

Stuart was now worried. He poured Tom a stiff drink and slowly reached for the remote and put it to one side. 'Come on mate - you're scaring me now. What's up?' Stuart placed his hand on Tom's shoulder and gave a gentle squeeze.

Tom's breathing started to return to normal - but he still had a scared look in his eyes. He explained to Stuart that a scene had popped up mid-credits, which he thought must have been a part of the film. A man in a red hoody was attacking another man. He stabbed him repeatedly until he collapsed and bled out. He recognised the man.

'Who? Who was the man?' Stuart asked, removing his hand from Tom's shoulder as if needing it back to concentrate on the story.

'It was - it was me!' Tom's voice broke a little.

Stuart tried to reassure Tom that there was no scene. He'd imagined it - he had after all, just watched some horrific death scenes where the antagonist specialised in stabbing his victims to death with knives attached to his glove. He suggested that Tom was tired and it was possible to drift off and dream a whole dream, that seemingly lasts for ages, within a few seconds of real time, before snapping out of it. 'Let's look at it rationally. If the scene was there — we'd have found it by now. We've rewound and played the credits about ten times now. There is no scene'.

Tom seemed somewhat reassured but he was sure he'd seen himself as an older man on the screen. He'd watched his own death.

For the next few weeks, Tom didn't go into work. He thought he recognised the road in the video as the one outside his flat. There was no way he was going near it — but there was no way of getting to work without crossing it. By week three, Tom had decided to leave the flat and head to work. He approached the road cautiously. He scanned his surroundings over and over again — but nobody was around. Tom took a big breath in and slowly exhaled. He crossed the road. A cyclist shot by and Tom jumped out of his skin. He had to regain his breath for a moment and reassure himself that he was being ridiculous. As he took a few more steps he saw a figure approaching. A male, definitely a male, and walking fast. 'Oh God' whispered Tom. The male was in a red hoody. Tom had a panic attack right there and then. He'd never experienced anything like it. He ran back across the road — a car screeched to halt, narrowly avoiding impact. Tom jumped the gate to the flats, fumbled frantically for his keys clumsily dropping them to the ground. 'No no no!', he cried. He grabbed the keys and jammed the front door key at the keyhole, missing a few times until it finally found its target. He threw the door open and slammed it shut. He leaned back against the door breathing rapidly. He turned to look out of the peep hole, and saw the man in the red hoody walk slowly past his gate. *Why was he now walking slowly? Why was he walking so quickly, then slowing down at his flat? It was him! It was him! Wasn't it?*

Tom began to isolate himself. Weeks turned to months, and months to years. He no longer answered phone calls from concerned friends and family. The doctor had to make a house call and diagnosed Tom with Agoraphobia. Tom couldn't work. He claimed benefits and had food delivered to the flat. He felt safe indoors.

Years turned to decades, until Tom finally reached retirement age. He thought about how the version of himself he'd seen in the footage was much younger than he was now - meaning, maybe he was now safe. He'd averted his death. By this time, times had moved on. We had broadband, google, and smartphones. Tom plucked up the courage to do some searching online for any reports of people experiencing the same thing. No results were found. But he did find a chat room dedicated to the paranormal. People in the chat room discussed their inexplicable experiences. There were people who'd been abducted by Aliens. People who'd seen ghosts. People that had had sex with ghosts. People who thought *they* were ghosts. People who'd been chased by Bigfoot. You name it - someone had been through it. Tom posed his question in one of the forums and closed his laptop. Days passed. Weeks passed. Until one day, he received a notification via email telling Tom he'd received a reply to his post.

Tom logged on. He prayed for something that would help put an end to his misery. He hoped he could finally start living his life — what little was left of it. He'd lived a life of loneliness and fear.

A rational explanation — a scientific explanation, was all he wanted. He'd be able to leave the flat — make friends, and maybe even find companionship — find love.

He logged into the forum.

'*1 unread message*'

Tom clicked on the message. The sender's username made Tom recoil in terror. He didn't dare click on the message. He rubbed his eyes and checked the name again. He wasn't mistaken. He'd mentioned no details regarding what the attacker was wearing in his post — yet the sender's name was: RedHoody69.

Tom took a big breath in, and clicked on the message, opening it. The message simply read:

"Oh Good - you're still there. Don't worry, I can wait"

"Faithfully,
Red Hoody69"

Tom fell to the floor, into the foetal position, and sobbed uncontrollable like a baby.

VR

8

Kyle Thornton - 49 years of age, woke up on Monday morning feeling pretty low. He was having one of his episodes. He'd been diagnosed with depression when he was a teenager and hadn't managed to ever truly get a handle on it. Mondays were always the worst. He rarely had the strength to motivate himself to drag himself out of bed. *What was the point?*

So Kyle did what he often did — called in sick. After lying in bed staring at the ceiling for a few hours, he thought to himself, *why do I bother? Is this all there is? There must be more than this.* Kyle cried. He felt ridiculous doing so, but he cried nonetheless.

Another couple of hours passed. He thought about his life and the lack of achievement. He thought about missed opportunities and how much time he'd wasted doing nothing but wallow.

On Tuesday, Kyle went into work. He had a pile of documents on his desk waiting for him. Kyle's job was data entry — a job he'd taken when he was 28 as a temporary job whilst he figured out what he wanted to do with his life. He never figured it out. The financial problems Kyle lived with were never going away. The only relationship he'd ever had ended before it had chance to blossom. It wilted and died.

Kyle felt like a complete loser. Nothing ever worked out and all of his friends had gone on to bigger and better things, leaving him behind.

On the way home from work that day, Kyle stood calmly waiting for his train. The next train wasn't stopping at the station. An announcement came over the public speaker system:

"The next train does not stop at this station — please stand back from the platform edge"

The train approached at speed and Kyle very casually stepped out in front of it. The train screeched to a halt and the commuters all stood aghast — a scream was heard, and a lot of 'Oh My Gods' could be heard. There were a lot of hands over mouths, parents shielding their children's eyes, and a traumatised train driver with blood and guts splattered all over his windscreen — then darkness.

A giant message appeared out of nowhere, then darkness.

"GAME OVER"

Kyle opened his eyes. The 'Game over' message faded before his eyes. *'Game over? Game over? What the fuck?'*.

Kyle looked straight ahead at the various multicoloured flashing lights, and the cacophony of ringing, beeps, alarms, and music, took a minute to sink in. He felt something uncomfortable pressing on his temples, and he quickly grabbed whatever it was and ripped it off.

'Hey hey hey! Watch it! Those NIs (neuro-interfaces) cost an arm and a leg,' came an irate voice.

A man appeared in front of Kyle, wearing a blue uniform with a logo of a star and the words 'Star Arcade'.

'Hey there fella, give it a second it'll all come back to you'. The voice had calmed and was now reassuring.

'Where am I? Am I dead? What is this?' Kyle was breathing rapidly, the panic in his voice led the uniformed man to place his hand on Kyle's shoulder. 'It's ok - here, take this'. The man held out a red pill. Kyle didn't care what it was, but if it helped with this overwhelming plethora of emotions, he'd take it. Kyle popped the pill and swallowed.

Gradually, the deafening sounds seemed to settle and the flashing lights weren't as blinding as they were seconds before.

A boy stood in front of him, no older than 14. 'Hey Kyle, hurry up and snap out of it will ya - I want to go again!'

Kyle stared at the boy for a few seconds, and his expression turned to one of confusion. His eyes suddenly widened and he stuttered, 'T-t-t-Toby?'

'Yeah man - come on hurry up!'

Kyle looked down at his hands, they were small. He looked at his feet, small. His hands were smooth and soft. 'What the fuck! Show me a mirror' demanded Kyle.

'What?' The boy asked.

'A mirror! A fucking mirror!' Snapped Kyle.

'Ok Ok - jeez' replied the boy.

The boy held out a device that resembled a phone. He pointed the screen at Kyle, which reflected his image back at him; and there stood a teenage boy; short and skinny — and wearing the oddest clothes. Kyle gasped.

'You boys seem to have this in order. Don't worry lad, for some people it takes a little longer. Maybe don't go quitting the game so traumatically next time' said the uniformed man, chuckling to himself before walking off.

'You're — you're - Toby?'

'Yeah we've established that' Toby replied, not paying much attention now — instead checking his fancy phone.

'I'm, Kyle' said Kyle.

'Oh for God's sake' Toby muttered.

Kyle scanned his surroundings. The room was massive and resembled an arcade — but he only recognised some of the machines — the rest looked alien to him.

10 more minutes passed and Kyle sat at a table eating a burger and laughing with Toby.

'Oh my god that was crazy!' Said Kyle excitedly. 'I was an old man!'

'Yeah you fucked up big time man. I've never seen such a low score! You didn't do anything!' Toby laughed uncontrollable. He was in hysterics.

'Hey, fuck off. I didn't have enough credits to pay for the expansion pack! I had to start from nothing! You started off with rich parent's and they bought you a fucking Ferrari for your 17th birthday! I got nothing!' Kyle responded defensively.

'Yeah well I heard Lucy McKay started from nothing and she ended up running a billion pound company and solving world hunger' Toby baited Kyle.

'That's not true! No way! That game's too hard!' Kyle snapped.

'As soon as you turned down that girl in college, she was pretty, you capped your progress and lost serious XP dude' said Toby, mockingly. 'And you dropped out of college! Big no no! You missed all the bonus levels and side-missions too — what a waste man!'

'Ok ok! I know! Let's just go again eh. I'll remember to do it differently next time'

'You know you can't take your memories with you into the game - you'll probably end up doing the same thing'

'Not if you lend me some credits - I can pay for the expansion pack and start off as someone cool and rich!'

'Fine. But I don't know why you're playing the 21st century level - it's grim! Just hurry - place closes in an hour'

20 minutes later Kyle and Toby emerged. They'd played the multiplayer option. Toby had a smile on his face and Kyle was clearly annoyed.

'How did you manage to fuck that up?' Toby laughed again.

'You stole my wife and she bled me dry. I was depressed and died alone - really old I was - like, really really old!'

'You're just not cut out for 21st century life dude. To be fair, even as a rich player - I was bored as hell. I'm so over that game - what a shit time period to live in! Poor suckers'

'Yeah - what a shit time. What the hell was that pandemic? Didn't know that happened. I was definitely born in the right century' Kyle laughed.

Kyle tapped his phone - a portal opened directly in front of him leading to his kitchen at home 25 miles away, where his mother was serving food. 'What time do you call this? And what have I told you about publicly opening portals directly into our house!'

'Sorry, Mum; I was playing *Twenty-first century*' said Kyle apologetically.

'That thing will rot your brain! Why would you want to visit that god awful time period? Just sit down' his Mum replied sternly.

'Sorry' Kyle replied.

'And close that bloody portal — you've got the whole bloody arcade staring in!'

'Hey Mrs Thornton!' Toby waved from the other side of the portal, still in the arcade.

'Hi Toby. Get yourself home, flower'

'Yes, Mrs T'. Toby winked, and the portal closed.

Kyle's Mum sat down at the table, as did Kyle.

'You should try the twenty-seventh century — now that's where it all happened!' Kyle's Mum said, pointing her knife towards Kyle as she spoke.

Suddenly, Kyle's Mum grasped her chest and fell to the floor. Kyle jumped down to the floor and grabbed her shoulders. 'Mum! Mum! Wake up! Mum, please!'

Everything went dark. The words,

"GAME OVER" appeared and faded.

Big Bad

9

Once upon a time, a little girl found herself wandering through the woods, lost and afraid. Not afraid of the dark, or afraid of what lurked in the shadows, but afraid she wouldn't make it home in time for supper. She was quite a big round girl and her parents' spoiled her and gave in to her every demand - demands that were usually food-orientated.

As she bounced along through the woods, looking for a tree that she recognised so as to piece together her route home, she heard a noise. She shouted, 'Who's there? Come out - I can hear you!'. Then came the noise again. The little girl looked down and realised it was her tummy. It was growling out for food. She felt rather silly about the fright, but then;

Upon her path she met a wolf.

'Greetings, little girl. How are you on this beautiful evening?' said the wolf with a smile.

'Quite well thank you, Mr Wolf'

'You look lost' said the wolf, seemingly concerned.

'I am. I need to get home for supper'

'It's getting dark little girl. I will take you home. I know these woods like the back of my paw' said the wolf.

'Thank you kind wolf' Said the girl.

As they walked together through the woods, they arrived at the border between the woods and her parent's farm.

'Here we are' said the wolf, 'Only two or three minutes from home. You can get your supper now'. The wolf smiled again.

'But I'm hungry now' replied the plump girl, licking her lips.

'You are close now. I can smell the hot food' said the wolf with a worried look in his eyes, uncertain of the podgy girl's wicked intentions.

'I think I'll have a snack on my way' said the girl.

The large little girl opened her knapsack and reached in.

'Oh you have snacks with you!' Said the wolf, relieved.

'No, just this machete' said the girl, holding up the sharp metal blade.

The greedy girl brought down her weapon with one foul-swoop and beheaded the wolf. She dropped to the ground almost as quickly as the wolf had, and buried her face in his carcass, biting chunks of flesh from the wolf. She devoured the whole wolf, even the bones.

The stuffed big little girl walked into her parents' cottage, where they waited at the dining table.

'What time do you call this?' said her mother.

'Your food is going cold — sit down!' snapped her father.

'I'm sorry Mama, papa - I got a little lost in the woods. What's for supper?' enquired the girl.

'Wolf' replied her mother.

'Aww shit' said the girl.

Naughty or nice

10

He's making a list, he's checking it twice
He's gonna find out, who's naughty or nice.

Adam and Claire were placing the last of the gifts under the tree. They placed a mince pie and a glass of Sherry on the mantelpiece. They put out the children's letters to Santa thanking him for coming. And finally, they fitted the trip-wires, greased the kitchen floor, and set down a few chunky metal bear traps — you know the kind; heavy metal clamps with razor-sharp spikes that slam shut when stepped on, piercing the flesh around the ankle and embedding into bone, often fracturing it badly.

'That should stop the fat bastard' said Claire with a grin.

Adam reached down into a chest near the Christmas tree and retrieved his trusty shotgun. He pumped the shotgun once, then took a seat in his armchair.

'And I'll be waiting' said Adam with a sinister smirk.

'There's no way that fat piece of shit is taking our children's gifts again this year' Claire responded, whilst reaching into the chest and retrieving a carving knife. Nobody knew why Claire and Adam had a weapons chest; and nobody asked.

Now why are these two perfectly ordinary (apart from the weapons chest that is) suburban parents plotting to take down Santa Claus on Christmas Eve? Well, let me explain.

Santa doesn't deliver presents. I'm sorry to break that to you but he doesn't. However, he is very real. *So why does he visit every house on Christmas Eve?* — I hear you ask. Well, it's to take away your presents. You see, Santa has a list of all the good children, and another list of all the bad children. He doesn't really need to visit the good children, as he doesn't have any presents for them, their parents can buy their own fucking presents, Santa isn't a charity. But Santa does expect food and drink — and it isn't wise to disappoint him. And it is true, he likes to eat mince pies and drink whatever shite you've left out for him — he's a greedy fat bastard like that. But the bad children, well, he will not only eat your food and drink your booze, but he'll also take away their presents, If they've been naughty that is; he has a list remember. And in place of the confiscated presents, he leaves coal; a lump of coal for every gift. *What gives him the right? What gives him the right to take away gifts I've bought my kids - I've spent a fortune on those gifts! And even if my kid has been naughty — that's none of your fucking business Santa.* Well, he's making it his fucking business.

Now I've educated you about Santa - let's return to Adam and Claire.

Adam and Claire Jones had two children, Jeremy and Jemima. For years the little shits had caused chaos in the village, running around doing whatever they pleased completely unsupervised. They'd loiter and litter, steal apples from peoples' apple trees on their private property, play truant, and incinerate poor little innocent bugs with a magnifying glass. And every year, Santa would come and take away their Christmas presents. Well, Adam and Claire had had enough, as had the children. Regardless of how much the kids misbehaved, they still loved their children — they were only 7 years old; twins if you were wondering.

So Adam and Claire set out to protect the gifts they'd spent their hard-earned cash on. And not only did they want to protect the presents, they wanted to take care of Santa Claus once and for all. Why nobody had thought of it before was beyond them.

Adam sat in his armchair and Claire slipped away into the bedroom, switching all the lights off as she left. Adam would sit in the chair waiting for Santa, shotgun at the ready.

Santa didn't come down the chimney — he used a crowbar to get through the window in the hallway by the front door. Sometimes he'd just jam it into the frame and pry it open, but if he couldn't be arsed, he'd just smash the glass and use his dark magic to silence the noise.

So in came Santa at 11:33pm on Christmas Eve. Adam heard some crashing about and a smash. *'He must have slipped on the greasy floor and landed on the shards of broken glass they'd put down'* thought Adam. He heard another bang and crash followed by a booming voice that sounded like the word 'bollocks!'. You couldn't see for the dark, but Adam was smiling. Santa regained his composure and made his way into the living room. A loud snap, a clunky smashing together of metal on bone 'Fuck!' Came the voice. Adam flipped a switch and the lights came on, revealing to Santa a devious Adam pointing a shotgun at his big fat jolly belly. 'Seasons Greetings Santa' said Adam, who had come up with a better line, but had forgotten it at the last minute and had to improvise.

'Hello Adam' said Santa, rather calmly, considering a bear trap had slammed shut piercing his ankle as easy as a knife through butter, which was spurting out Santa blood all over the carpet.

'You're not going near these presents. You're not going anywhere' Adam tried to speak with confidence, but found his voice was breaking somewhat; Santa's presence did tend to instil fear.

'Oh My Boy - I'm not here for the presents — the children have been good this year. Surely you noticed?' Said Santa.

'What? Well, no. Th-th-then wh-wh-what are you doing here?' Adam enquired, his voice a little more submissive, his childhood stutter returning.

'May I help myself to this mince pie, and is this, sherry? Smells delightful!' Santa smiled.

'Oh. Right. Of c-c-course' Adam replied.

Santa dragged his lame leg still firmly stuck in the bear trap, over to the fireplace and picked up his treats. Suddenly, Claire appeared and lunged for Santa. She slammed the carving knife deep into his throat, 'What the hell is going on Adam - why is he still breathing?' Claire's voice trembled.

'It's ok love — put the knife down' Adam placed the shotgun down, resting it against the side of the chair, and held out both hands, palms facing forward, in a surrendering gesture.

'You heard the man, Claire'. Santa grabbed the carving knife wedged into his neck - Claire still held the handle, Santa held the blade, which cut into his hand causing blood to slide down the blade, the blade handle, and both Santa's and Claire's hands and wrists. She pulled away, leaving Santa with the knife. He yanked out the blade from his neck, his carotid artery spurting out blood everywhere. Her breathing was heavy and her eyes wide with fear. She was confused and terrified by this man. Santa demolished his mince pie and downed his booze. He threw the knife at the fairy on the tree, thrusting it from the top of the tree and impaling the poor little fairy into the wall. He then reached down and pried open the bear-trap with his bare hands, cutting into them again. He didn't even wince.

'Are you two quite finished?' Santa spoke like an irritated school teacher telling off a pair of naughty kids. Naughty kids who'd just tried to murder him.

'Y-yeah. We're so s-s-sorry. We thought you were here for the gifts. You can go - it's fine' Adam pleaded.

'Oh I can leave can I? I'm free to go am I? Well, that's very charitable of you' Santa's sarcasm scared the couple. His voice was growing deep and insidious.

'No - we only meant-' interrupted Claire.

'Silence!' Santa bellowed. 'Your children have been well behaved, I will not take their toys'.

'Oh thank you — thank you Santa' cried Claire.

'I won't take their toys because it is not they who were naughty' came Santa's response.

'What? You mean — us?' Adam's fear turned to confusion.

'Yes, you. Both of you have been very naughty' Santa grinned a sinister grin.

'Naughty? We're good christians. We pay our taxes, give to charity, look after our children. We're good people! How dare you?' snapped Clare.

'I might be getting this all wrong — but did you not just try to murder Santa? Is Santa's ankle shattered? Does Santa have a nasty laceration over his hand? Is blood oozing from Santa's neck?'.

'Oh no — we were only trying to protect our children. It was self-defence! It was-'

'Don't waste your breath Claire' Adam interjected whilst reaching for the shotgun he'd rested down by the side of his chair. He can't do shit. We're not children. I still have a shotgun. And we don't have any presents he can take from us' said Adam, feeling smug about his logic.

'Oh, I take presents because they're precious to the children. Everybody has something precious to them. I don't need to take toys or Playstations, or dolls; just whatever happens to be precious to you. Right, I'd better be off — still a few million houses left, and I've already spent too long with you two idiots. - Merry Christmas Adam. Merry Christmas Claire' Adam aimed the shotgun and fired, but Santa vanished, which was a bit weird considering he'd had to crow bar his way into the property.

'Adam, what does he mean? Precious? What's he going to do?' Claire's voice trembled once more.

'Oh my God! The children!' cried Adam.

The parents raced upstairs like olympic hurdlers, jumping three steps at a time. Once they'd conquered the stairs, Adam slammed open the door to the children's room. There were two beds, one blue and one pink. Both were neatly made with the duvets folded like a napkin. On each pillow there sat a lump of coal in place of each child.

Santa was a vengeful bastard.

But on the plus side, he'd left the gifts, which included a PS4 and a Nintendo Switch. 'Thank God for small mercies' thought Adam. Claire sobbed — the kids would need replacing and she didn't like the idea of having to give birth again.

Ronald's Garden

11

Ronald looked up at the sky and wondered how he'd ended up lying on the ground, covered in dirt.

Actually, forget it — the twist is that Ronald is a garden rake. It's a bit like Pete's garden but with a rake instead of a potato. Ronald the Rake? Forget it. Forgive me; writer's block; it's lockdown. Never mind.

The Prisoner

12

John Barker was woken by an alarm. Not a pleasant alarm by any stretch of the imagination — but the loud, beeping of an old bedside alarm clock, 'beep beep beep beep beep beep beep beep'. He found himself in a room, a modest sized room but big enough for a single bed in the corner. It was painted white all over with a single lightbulb hanging from the ceiling — no light cover, shade or pendent, or whatever you'd call it. The square room had one door painted white, with a brass handle, the only thing allowing it to stand out as a door. An unassuming wooden table and chair, again painted white, had been placed in the centre of the room. On it, a meal; steak and chips, with a glass of water. Unnervingly, somebody had dressed John in pyjamas, which he'd found quite disturbing since he had no recollection of dressing himself in pyjamas.

John had committed the heinous crime of protesting against the greed of wealthy landlords driving up prices in the rental market and driving the poor farther and farther away from their home towns and cities. Unless you already had wealth — buying a house was impossible for the majority. John and thousands of others had gathered outside parliament to protest this — despite protests being outlawed in the early 2030s. The movement blamed the regime for allowing this and enabling the rich to get rich and the poor poorer. He remembered being herded up by riot police and hurled into the back of a van. He had no idea what happened to his fellow protestors but could only imagine they were waking up in similar circumstances. The rumours about how the regime dealt with those who openly criticised them were true.

John didn't want his meal. He wanted to go home. Maybe he could go home — because on the floor was a key, just lying there conspicuously. Maybe this was just a warning — next time there would be no key.

He picked up the key and tried the lock. It opened — *thank God*. The key was now jammed in the lock and John couldn't pull it back out, as hard as he tried.

The door was smaller than your average door, and John had to crouch down to exit the room. As he did so, the door slammed shut behind him, pushing him forward and into the new room. This room was even smaller than the last. He was already crouching and had to stay that way — this room had been made for someone much smaller, he thought. The room had a lower ceiling but also a smaller area to move around in. There was no table this time, but still a meal, this time, just baked beans, in a bowl, on the floor. A glass of water was placed next to the bowl — the water looked murky. *To hell with this,* thought John, who had already located another key and proceeded to another door on the opposite side of the room. He tried the lock and turned the key, opening the door. He couldn't see into the next room, there were no lights — it was pitch black. He hesitated, but decided to proceed. He'd feel his way out — the next key would inevitably be on the floor, and the door on the opposite side. The door slammed behind him and suddenly the lights came on. The door controlled the lights in a way completely opposite to a fridge door; the light came on when the door closed, not the other way around.

This room was smaller still — and John yelled profanities at the ceiling as if shouting at God.

There was bread on the floor, no plate, some murky water and a key next to it. Nothing more.

John simply had to get out of there. Even if he had to go through every room in the building.

John went from one room to the next, each smaller and more bleak than before. He wanted to know whether the next room would be an improvement on the previous — but the darkness of the room until the door slammed left him unable to make that assessment. He had an idea.

John opened the next door, but this time, removed his pyjama top, and wedged it between the door and doorframe, so that he could feel his way around the room, get an idea of it's dimensions and contents, before deciding whether or not he should stay, proceed, or return to his previous room. As he felt his way in the dark and navigated the room, he heard the slamming of the door and the lights came on. The door had closed and the pyjama top was gone. The room had a high ceiling but was no bigger than a very small bathroom. He picked up the key and went over to the previous door. This key wouldn't fit the lock, evidently only designed to open the exit door, and not the entry door.

John grew more and more anxious and despondent — he'd been at it for over an hour now, and wasn't any closer, as far as he was aware, to getting out. There was no food or drink in this room — but this one had a bedpan — something missing from the previous rooms, and something he hadn't considered up until this point. He had no choice but to try the next room, unless he'd planned to starve to death after taking the shit he'd inevitably need to take at some point.

John crawled through the next door; thinking to himself how demeaning it was having to crawl through what felt like a cat flap.

The light came on. Success! This room was much bigger — bigger than all those that had come before. There was a table on which rested platters of food from a variety of cultures. A jug of water and a bottle of Malbec, his favourite, stood proudly on the table top. An actual flushable toilet had been installed in the corner of the room. It wasn't sealed off, but there was nobody else in the room to stare at him taking a shit — so he was just grateful it wasn't a bed pan. There was a two-seater sofa in another corner, and a single bed in another. This was luxury in comparison to the previous rooms, but this was the mind game being played, thought John; they wanted him to give up. The key was left in full sight by the wine glass next to the Malbec. John took a seat and shovelled the food into his mouth, gulped down the water, and poured himself a glass of red.

Despite John knowing this was all a mind game and a punishment — he still couldn't bear the thought of leaving the room — the thought of finding himself in another small room made his stomach hurt and a headache grow. John took a seat on the sofa and gradually drifted away.

John awoke refreshed and resolute in his determination to escape. The table had been cleared from the night before, and now a full continental breakfast awaited. John ate and drank a glass of orange juice quickly, before picking up the key and marching over to the door.

Unsurprisingly, the room was smaller and less hospitable than the previous, but John had a renewed purpose and knew he had to keep going.

One room after another, the space grew smaller and smaller. Again, he found himself in a room barely big enough for a dog. After this room came a bigger room, then a smaller room, a smaller room still, and a bigger room.

Days turned to weeks and John had tried to spot patterns that didn't exist. Some days he would resign himself to a comfortable room and stay for days, and some days he would keep going until exhaustion and despair kicked in, and sleep in whatever room he happened to be in.

One day, a bearded, dishevelled looking John, entered yet another room. It was big. It had a separate bathroom; finally, he could take a dump in a room that wasn't also the kitchen, dining room and bedroom combined. There were books, flowers, a fridge and freezer, an oven and stove, a wardrobe full of clothes, a bed with clean sheets, and a comfortable sofa. And toilet roll! He'd missed toilet roll — wiping his arse had become a challenge and involved sacrificing some of his drinking water for washing his arse; which ran down his legs and onto the floor, or sometimes directly into the bedpan — which looked suspiciously like the murky water he'd been drinking up until now. The room was spacious enough — much like a hotel room with a double bed; nicely sized, but too much crammed in; you wouldn't want to be stuck in there every day.

The room had three doors this time! This was it — the final test! John had no idea how long he'd been in this prison but knew he wanted out. Over each door knob, hung a key on a string. Above each door was a different word. Door one simply read, 'Luxury'; door two read, 'Smaller'; and door three, 'Freedom'.

John was tired. So very tired. He'd spent weeks, maybe months, playing their mind games, drinking their dirty water, and shitting on the floor like a dog. He'd gone without food for days at a time, frantically bouncing from one room to the next, sweating and sobbing, but never giving up. And now, now was the ultimate test. John had lost count of how many times he'd thought to himself, 'this is the one, the true test' before realising it was just another room. But he'd never seen this room before — this one had three doors. It truly was the final test. He allowed himself to feel excited — hopeful even. He vowed to himself a long time ago that he would never give up until he was free, but he'd become tired and despondent, and such vows lose their worth during times of crisis. He knew that the next room, whichever he chose, would be the final destination — there would be no further doors — he'd be stuck with whatever came next. Suddenly, the choice was harder than it had ever been before. John feared going back to one of the tiny bleak rooms he'd spent time in, with murky water, marmite, and not even a pot to piss in. He feared losing this room — he'd never had it so good in here, and the thought of gambling it for something more scared the shit out of him . We're talking anxiety levels usually only experienced by fighter pilots, brain surgeons, astronauts, and those of us on our twelfth cup of coffee by midday. He was absolutely shitting it. He weighed his options. If there is any honesty in this whole situation, it should be that there is indeed one luxurious room, one smaller room than the one in which he currently resided, and finally, one room that leads to his freedom. That's assuming honesty that is. What John had to determine was whether the honesty extended to the accurate labelling of the doors. Were they aptly named? Surely not? So, John thought on. Two of the doors would lead to an improvement in his circumstances; namely, freedom, or luxury. One door, would lead to a worsening of his situation, namely, 'smaller'. The mind game was still playing — obviously the doors could be labelled incorrectly, but that's exactly what they want him to think. So maybe they're labelled correctly. Maybe the door marked 'Luxury' really was a luxurious room brimming with decadence and splendour. Or was it a double-bluff? They know he'll be cynical and suspect deception, so maybe they'll mark the doors accurately, knowing he won't believe them. But that's exactly what they want him to think! Of course they know that he knows they're trying to play tricks, and they know he'll try and second guess them. John could not think straight — he was trying so hard to figure out how his captor's minds worked and how to beat them, that he forgot about one possibility — one outcome he hadn't considered: they could all be shit! All three rooms could be small, shitty little pits of despair he'd have to spend the rest of his days in — drinking his own piss and eating marmite fucking sandwiches. No - he couldn't let this happen. His body deflated — his initial excitement at the prospect of escape, or at the promising odds that his situation would be improved by picking one of the three doors, dwindled and faded to black. His despair was palpable in the sweat pouring down his brow, or the clamminess of his hands. He knew that's exactly the sort of torture they'd already subjected him to — he'd get his hopes up, then find himself in a tiny little shoebox for eternity. John wanted freedom, but he'd be grateful for any improvement. One thing he couldn't bear the thought of, was a worse room. He wanted things to not get worse, more than he wanted his freedom. And when John realised this, his decision was made. He sat on his little sofa, pulled a book off the shelf, swung his legs up onto one of the cushions, and began to read to himself.

John spent the rest of his long, long life in that room.

What rooms were behind each door you say? There were no rooms behind each door. Each door led to exactly the same place; freedom. The doors were visible from the street and thousands of people passed by every day. People rarely notice innocuous doors. How many doors have you walked past, that you couldn't figure out why it was there or where it led? More than you know. We walk past weird things all the time — but are quite happy to think, *that's weird,* before putting it to the back of our minds and carrying on with whatever it was we were doing. Well, many tourists and many locals walked past three weirdly placed, side by side, innocuous doors, but they never let their curiosity turn into investigation. If they had, they'd have found on the other side, an innocuous man in his pyjamas, eating steak and drinking wine.

The Cursed Stones

13

Alex and William lived next to the cemetery. A lot of kids are scared of such places — but not these two, they were used to it being there — it was always there, so they thought nothing of it. In fact, Alex and William saw it as just another playground. But a cemetery is not a playground — something Alex and William would soon find out.

Alex was 9 and William 10. They both went to the same school and lived just 3 doors away from each other. They spent every possible waking hour playing together, for they were best friends.

The boys would often climb over the cemetery bars — a dangerous task in itself, as they were tall and pointy They'd run around the graves playing games. Disrespectful? Maybe. Dangerous? Definitely. For spirits do not take kindly to their resting places being disturbed by children — and neither do the visitors — who would often complain to the council about 'youths' loitering in the graveyard causing trouble and disrespecting the graves of their loved-ones.

But all they wanted to do was play-they meant no harm or disrespect. They hadn't even stopped at any point to consider what a place like this meant to anyone. They just saw it as somewhere to play, and somewhere a bit spooky, which made it cool in their eyes. So they played. They played conkers when it was conker season. There was only one conker tree worthy of their attention and it was huge! They could see it from their homes and its branches overarched the railings of the cemetery. When they weren't happy with the conkers that nature had dropped at their feet, they would hurl the biggest and heaviest stick they could find into the branches of the 'conker tree' (having never heard of a horse chestnut tree) knocking unsuspecting conkers to the ground below. The bigger the conker, the more delighted the child. There were lots of trees, and they would climb as many as were climbable. When it was hot and sunny, they would fill up their empty washing up liquid bottles - or 'squirty bottles' as they charmingly called them - with water from the tap used by visitors to water the flowers. Here they were, visiting their dear departed, whilst two little urchins ran around blasting each other with water from squirty bottles. When the sun began to set, hide and seek began. Often other kids from the neighbourhood would join Alex and William when it got dark - they loved the thrill of hiding in a graveyard at night. The idea was to hide and not get caught - but the actual joy came from getting caught - as if you did it well, you could scare the living shit out of the person catching you. So in the end, it wasn't actually hard to find the hiders — the seeker just had to wander around the graveyard in the dark and wait for each and every hider to take his or her turn jumping out from behind a grave or from a bush, or down from a tree. Nobody wanted to be the seeker — as it was just an evening dedicated to surviving multiple heart attacks. It's a good job they were kids — if they were as old as you or I, their hearts would have exploded.

One evening, after hide and seek, the two boys stood before a garage. Just a garage on its own — not attached to a house or anything — just a garage in a cemetery. They thought this was odd — but even more odd that they'd never seen it before. William felt uneasy about the garage, and how darker it had become. Normally they'd be home by the time it got this dark. They'd already been out too long — it was past their bedtime and the other children had all gone home. But Alex wanted to look around some more — he couldn't believe he'd not seen it before. He circled the garage, kicked the heavy metal door, which he could, even in the dark, make out to be green. It rattled for a few seconds after the kick — and it was a loud enough bang to make William jump. 'I'm going!' said William - taking a step back. 'Don't be a wimp' replied Alex.

Alex saw an opportunity to scare William. He told him a story his Grandad had once told him about a garage in a graveyard that once belonged to the caretaker, who disappeared years ago after a string of brutal murders in the cemetery. Legend has it, that he took children who played in the graveyard, tied them up, and put them in his garage. He would then drive in on his steamroller to crush them whilst they frantically tried to wriggle away, screaming at first in terror, and then in excruciating pain as the steamroller crushed them from the feet up, slowly, until their heads popped open, splashing the contents in a bloody red blast radius of about a metre, which the roller casually passed over, briefly concealing the atrocity.

'That's such bullshit!' William replied.

'It's true. I heard it from my Grandad and he knows all about this cemetery' Alex snapped back defensively, clearly annoyed that William had so rudely dismissed his lie as a lie.

'You looked just as surprised as I was to see a garage here — so how come all of a sudden you know it's story?' William cleverly interrogated.

'I was surprised. My Grandad said the garage was demolished over 20 years ago. It shouldn't be here anymore. They knocked it down and set fire to the rubble - with the caretaker still inside!' Alex tried to deliver his narrative in a scary voice but it didn't work on William, who was too busy picking his tall-tale apart.

'Hold on. You said the caretaker disappeared. Now you're saying he was burned alive - or crushed in the rubble - or something. What is it? Disappeared? Or killed?' William asked, tilting his head to one side and smiling smugly.

'The official story was that he disappeared. But the story told by the adults who still remember what happened that night, is that the locals knew what he'd done - and they took care of it themselves.' Alex looked back at the garage, 'Why haven't we seen it before?' He whispered to himself.

'Can we go now' William asked.

'Yeah, but first you have to take a green stone from one of the graves' said Alex. William looked confused.

Alex had seen green and red stones on various graves, and wondered what they were. They were glass chippings used decoratively on graves, often surrounding a flower pot, or filling the whole plot, encased in a marble border. But when he'd asked his Grandad what they were a few months ago, his Grandad told him more,

'They're powerful stones. They're there to protect the spirits of the dead — you must never take them. If they are removed from their graves, the stones become cursed and the one who stole them, will suffer' Alex's Grandad's eyes went wide and pierced Alex's soul.

'Suffer? How?' asked Alex, intrigued as well as scared.

'If you take a green stone — you'll be plagued by the most terrifying nightmares — so scary you may be scared to death'

'And what about the red ones?' Alex interjected.

'The red ones? The red ones bring death to your door'

'Death in the dream? Death inside the nightmare, Grandad?'

'No - not just inside the nightmare. These are red stones. The nightmare becomes real with red stones'

Alex gulped. 'How do you know about this?'

'I survived the stones after stealing some' replied grandad.

'How?'

'Well, - I had terrible nightmares, so I put them back on the grave I found them on'.

'So how do you know the red ones bring death?'

'Because I lost a good friend back then. Stay clear of those stones. I don't want you in that graveyard anymore lad'.

Alex gulped again. But he knew his Grandad liked to scare him with his stories — even Alex's Mum and Dad used to tell off Grandad for scaring him. 'That's not age appropriate' he'd hear them say, and Grandad would always reply, 'pish' or 'nonsense'.

Alex and William now stood over a huge grave. It was the biggest in the whole cemetery. It had chains around it, which they ignored and stepped over. The tombstone was tall and majestic. It was made of stone rather than marble, and the names and years of birth and death were barely legible, worn away over time by the elements, and covered by mould, moss, and fungi. Behind the tombstone, towering over it, was a statue of an angel, its wings spread, powerful and overbearing. It protected the grave, its hands resting protectively across the top of the tombstone. Even though its eyes were closed, the boys felt like it was watching them. They should hurry before it wakes up, thought William. In front of the tombstone, were thousands of stones; green ones. 'Go on, take one!' said Alex.

William picked up a green stone. It looked like a green emerald William thought, even though he'd never seen a green emerald in real life. William then mocked Alex for daring him to take one but not taking one himself. So Alex being Alex, took a green stone too.

To the left of the grave was another, less majestic, more modest grave. It had also been neglected, and the writing also hidden by moss. There was no angel protecting this one. But it was protected — by stones; red stones.

'Take one of those' said William.

'No. We've got the green ones. Don't need a red one too' Alex's voice trembled at the idea.

'Oh now who's scared? Bwark Bwaaaark' William not only made the chicken noises, but he did the chicken movements, flapping his elbows back and forth like chicken wings.

'Fine! Let's grab red stones too' Alex snapped — irritated by the chicken accusation.

Alex and William both leant down, and carefully plucked a red stone each. They popped their stones into their pockets and finally headed off home, mentally preparing themselves for the inevitable telling off they'd receive for staying out late.

After their respective tellings off, the boys went to their respective beds, in their respective bedrooms, in their respective houses. William put his stones under his pillow, not for any special reason, he just didn't want his parent's finding them and telling him off for playing in the cemetery again. Alex, left the stones in his trouser pockets, which he'd thrown on the floor in the corner of his bedroom. He'd pretty much forgotten he'd taken them as soon as he got home — he was so tired from the day's activities, that he was asleep as soon as his head hit the pillow.

At William's house — he laid in bed, tossing and turning, groaning and frowning. William was about to have a nightmare.

At Alex's house — he laid in bed, sweating, mumbling, and turning his head repeatedly from side to side. He too was about to have a nightmare.

Alex sat up suddenly, startled by a noise from outside. He got out of bed and walked over to the window, pulled the curtains open, and looked out. Something cold and dark sent shivers down his spine and his belly tightened up and filled with butterflies. He looked farther afield — towards the cemetery. A figure stepped out from the shadows and turned its head to look at Alex - who staggered back, nearly tripping over himself. Alex gasped. It was the angel statue. He blinked a slow blink, rubbed his eyes and looked again. The angel was gone. He sighed a sigh of relief. But before he'd had time to recover his breath, he felt a pull on his whole body — he was pulled at great speed through his closed window as if he were a ghost, flying through the air towards the cemetery — his heart pounded and he was filled with dread. Passing countless graves and trees he finally stopped at the angel statue — which was back to its normal state. Alex stepped back as he had done before, but the statue reached out with its right hand and seized his left wrist tightly. Alex tried to pull away in vain. The angel looked at Alex, into his soul, and slowly raised its left arm, turned it towards the adjacent grave, and pointed towards the blanket of red stones. Alex screamed but no noise came out. The angel released its grip and Alex snapped back to his bedroom as if attached to some invisible bungee rope, and landed on his bed. He sat bolt upright, opened his eyes and breathed heavier than he ever had before — his heart still pounding and his eyes wide open. He looked at his left wrist which was red and sore. He cried and cried until his Dad rushed into the room.

    Meanwhile, William opened his eyes and found himself stood in front of the garage in the cemetery. He tried to step back but couldn't move — he couldn't even move his head. The garage made a sound, like somebody kicked a metal dustbin — someone was trying to open it from the inside. William tried to scream but his mouth wouldn't open — instead a muffled sound came out — like somebody had stuffed a sock into his mouth. The garage began to open, slowly. The lower edge of the garage door was rising and rising and the dark opening was growing and growing., slowly revealing giant Doc Martens. William tried to scream again — but nothing came out. The opening garage door rose higher and higher, revealing legs and a waist, and a torso, arms and a neck, and finally a head. A dishevelled looking bearded man stood, barely visible in the darkness, dressed in dark blue overalls. It was the caretaker! Behind him was a steamroller. It was green with two big narrow wheels, one on each side towards the rear, and a narrow black chimney stood tall on the front — and the big roller wheel at the front was red with blood. The caretaker smiled with sinister intent, turned, and walked over to the rear of the machine where he climbed aboard. The engine roared and smoke bellowed from the beast. It started to move towards William, slowly. As it approached, William tried to pull away as hard as he could — but his feet felt glued to the ground, and his body was numb. The roller got close, so close that Will could smell the metal and almost taste the blood, when it suddenly stopped. The engine stopped growling, and the smoke dissipated. The caretaker leaned forward and pointed towards a grave, the grave with the red stones. Will woke up suddenly — he patted his body up and down in the bed, checking he could feel again, and then cried quietly and told himself it was just a nightmare. He sighed a sigh of relief, wiped the sweat from his brow, and felt the wet bedsheets beneath him.

Alex's Dad took him to the cemetery the very next morning to return the stones. His Dad had heard the same stories from his father when he was a child, but never believed them — but he did believe that stories had great power and could affect people — especially the young and impressionable. Alex slowly crouched and leaned in to return the red stone to its rightful place. He did the same with the green stone; looking up at the angel and quietly whispering 'I'm sorry'. And that was the end of it — for Alex.

The same day, Alex slept on the sofa, intermittently waking for a drink or to watch a cartoon - before falling asleep again, making up for the lack of sleep the night before. Nighttime came and Alex went to bed. He slept for an hour or two, before waking up suddenly, 'William!' Alex cried out William's name so loud, he worried he'd woken his parents. He thought about everything that had happened and how glad he was he'd returned the stones. But what really concerned him was William. He'd completely forgotten about William. He hadn't told him to return his stones. He hadn't even checked to see if he'd had a nightmare too. Alex jumped out of bed, threw on some clothes and sneaked out of the house as quiet as a mouse.

He ran as fast as he could to the graveyard — something told him to head straight there — that is where he would find his friend. He scoured the cemetery for 15 minutes, including the graves that had caused him such torment. It occurred to Alex that he hadn't checked the garage they'd discovered the day before. He ran at top speed until it was within sight. He was still some distance away but he was close enough. The garage door was open and William was lying down on his back, in the garage. Outside was a steamroller, occupied by the caretaker. The engine roared and the smoke bellowed from the chimney. The caretaker turned and looked at Alex and laughed a villainous laugh. If he'd had a moustache he'd have twisted it. Alex cried out, 'No! No! Leave him alone!'. The caretaker turned away and set his machine in motion. William wriggled and struggled — but he was restrained by some invisible force. He managed to tilt his head so that his chin touched his chest and his eyes looked forward to see the oncoming iron beast. His eyes bulged in terror, and this time, unlike the night before, he *was* able to scream. That scream penetrated Alex's body, mind, and soul. The scream grew louder and louder as the huge front roller crushed William's feet and legs. The screaming and crying continued longer than either boys could bear. Alex fell to the floor in tears. The roller continued, over William's pelvis, his abdomen, and finally chest, until only his head remained. His pain and suffering seemed to stretch out longer than it should be possible. His screaming was quieter now but his suffering hadn't dwindled. Now William was just a head, waiting to be crushed and quietened forever. The garage door closed of its own accord and William's final moment was left only to the imagination.

Alex managed to stand, and he ran towards the garage — no longer fearing it — but just wanting to get to his friend. A foggy mist appeared out of nowhere and the garage faded. When he reached out to the garage, there was no garage. On the floor was a red stone. Alex reached down and retrieved it. He took it back to its grave and placed it down gently. William's story could never be told - Alex would never be believed and nobody would ever find William. He was reported missing and his family would never find peace — always wondering what happened and if he was still out there. Alex carried a huge weight of guilt with him for the rest of his life. He never stepped foot into a graveyard ever again, even for his Grandad's funeral. At the wake, old photos of his Grandad throughout the years were displayed amongst flowers and sympathy cards. Alex looked closer and saw a man with his arm resting on a child's shoulder — he recognised the man. 'Who is this?' Alex asked his father, who replied, 'Why that's the old caretaker and your grandad when he was a boy'

'That uniform?' Alex said, stunned, 'I know that uniform'.

'Your grandad probably described him in great detail — he loved a good story. That caretaker used to pay the kids to help him with odd jobs — he was great with them. Your Great Grandad used to say the old caretaker was murdered in that cemetery and we found out he was a very bad man'.

'That's why they burned him?' asked Alex.

Alex's Dad was stunned, 'your Grandad told you that? They're just stories. Nonsense'.

Alex looked wide-eyed at his Father, 'No they aren't'. Alex's words sent chills down his Father's entire body, 'He's real. Alex peed himself again'.

Wake, work, sleep, repeat.

14

Jack woke up at 6am to his fucking alarm. He hated mornings and painfully struggled to get out of bed every fucking day. He hated that he had to work. He reasoned that because he had no choice but to work, his job was tantamount to slavery. He knew that wouldn't go down well with anybody at all, so he simply referred to his job as forced servitude.

His journey into work was just as traumatic as his waking up and getting out of bed experience. The tube was always packed and people pissed him off. He could never find a seat and people nudged him, poked him, prodded him, sneezed and coughed near him, and wouldn't move an inch to let him off at his stop.

At work, Jack walked over to his desk, always with a cup of coffee he'd picked up on his way in, and switched on his computer. He'd give perfunctory smiles and nods to his colleagues, occasionally throwing smalltalk their way, but generally kept himself to himself. His phone would ring and he would answer with the same greeting he'd answered with for years, and continued to do so for the rest of the day on another 60 to 70 calls. He'd answered with that greeting thousands of times. It pained him every single time. He'd applied for other jobs but never succeeded.

His salary was poor and his flat was tiny and ugly. They called it a studio flat which made it sound more respectable than what it actually was, a bedsit with a mould problem.

On his way home, Jack stood on the platform and waiting for his train, he stepped out, falling towards the tracks before being hit by a train. He exploded like a balloon full of ketchup dropped from the roof of a high-rise flat, hitting the concrete below at terminal velocity. Even some commuters on the platform got splashed with blood.

Jack woke up at 6am to his fucking alarm again. He struggled to rise and thought, 'what an awful dream' and thought it just typical his idea of a nightmare would be another shift at work. He now felt like he'd just finished work and now he had to go back to work for another shift. He was exhausted from dreaming about work and suicide.

His journey to work was just as it was in his dream. A commuter spoke on his mobile phone for the entire journey which irritated Jack perhaps more than it should have.

He got into work and answered about 80 calls that day. On his way home he stood on the platform waiting for the train. As it sped towards the station - Jack stepped back from the edge, remembering his nightmare and feeling a little uneasy about it.

Jack went home, had a pretty shitty microwave meal, watched some YouTube videos for about 3 hours, then went to bed and slept.

The next morning, Jack was woken by his fucking alarm again. He hated mornings. He struggled to get out of bed.

Jack continued to do this for another two weeks until it occurred to him that he'd died the day he stepped into the path of that train, and had since gone to hell. His own personal Hell. He decided to test his theory and headed to the train platform.

The ugly duckling

15

Nigel was ugly. There were no two ways about it; he was objectively ugly. Even on the inside, he apparently had no redeeming characteristics. The schoolboys and girls were cruel towards him and he was cruel in return. They called him horrible names and he lashed out at them in return. He would hurt them badly — deliberately trying to scar them so that they would be ugly too. He knew he looked different, and the way he was cruelly scorned by the people, created cruelty within him that rivalled and even surpassed theirs.

As he grew older, people became kinder and compassionate, which tempered his anger and resentment. He realised kids were cruel but adults tended to be more understanding and kind; even though they still stared and pointed, at least they tried to do it discretely. He went from misanthropist to philanthropist over the course of nine or ten years, setting up a charity which helped provide counselling services to people disfigured in accidents or because of birth defects. He really wanted to help those who felt alone or different. Nigel had changed — he was now a good man.

Nigel even met someone. Her name was Tara. She was a volunteer at the charity and had once received counselling herself, thanks to the charity. She now worked for him and they understood each other. They'd both been subjected to the same taunting and torment that came with their appearances. Tara was very happy. She'd only ever had a handful of boyfriends before Nigel but she hadn't been sexually gratified by them, something unbearable to someone with a healthy and unapologetic sexual appetite. Why should men boast about being sexually charged and be so proud of their conquests whilst women remain reserved? She'd only had a few boyfriends but would not apologise for wanting someone more attentive and able in the bedroom. Nigel however, was hung like a donkey and she loved every inch of it. Nigel used to go to the gym and in the showers he would proudly show off his exceptional appendage. Other men would stare in disbelief — and Nigel liked that nobody was looking at his face in disgust, they were too busy looking at his third leg in envy.

As Nigel left the gym one evening, he saw a beautiful woman standing on the opposite side of the road waiting to cross. She was everything instagram and glamour magazines had brainwashed him into thinking was attractive. A man walked up and stood alongside Nigel. They both waited for the green man, and neither men could take their eyes off the woman. Then Nigel noticed the man; he was young and handsome, with a strong jaw and an air of confidence that made Nigel uneasy. Perhaps he was one of those instagram influencers or something. His hair was immaculate and his skin unblemished. His dress sense was impeccable and his smile could disarm an army of instagram followers.

As they crossed the road, Nigel was curious as to how the two beautiful people would interact. Would it be a glance and a smile, or would one of them speak to the other — good looking people had the confidence to do that sort of thing right? As they were about to pass each other Nigel noticed she wasn't looking at the good-looking guy to his left, she was looking at him, and it wasn't the usual look of disgust or disdain, it was attraction, — physical attraction! She looked at him seductively and gently bit her bottom lip. It was surreal! He'd never experienced anything like it. He'd seen others receive such looks, but he'd never been on the receiving end. Even his girlfriend wasn't physically attracted to his face, she simply enjoyed his company and his body. She had quite the sexual appetite and this trumped his appearance. Nigel got to the other side of the pavement, paused, and looked back to the other side confusedly, but she was gone.

'Feels good right?'

'Huh?' Replied Nigel.

The good-looking man had stopped and was now facing Nigel.

'The feeling — the feeling you get when you feel desired. It's good right?'

'Well, yeah — amazing. Sorry, who are you?' said Nigel, still feeling slightly caught off guard.

'Just a friend' came the reply, along with the disarming smile.

'Oh God - you're a weirdo aren't you. Well, I'm off. Nice chatting. Please don't follow me'

'Nigel, you've changed a lot since you were young. I'm proud of you. Your charity is amazing. You're a good man.' The stranger sounded fatherly — but Nigel never knew his father.

'How do you know who I am? What is happening here?' Nigel was showing his frustration, but the stranger kept smiling.

'How would you like to have that feeling all the time? How would you like to be desired by women - all women?' The man sounded serious and his smile had gone. 'I'll allow you this, a reward for your good behaviour. If you wish to be better looking - It shall be so. But I warn you - there are no gains without sacrifice. This is no lie - it's simple - you wish - you get'. The stranger stood waiting for an answer.

Nigel laughed so hard he silently farted, before finally regaining his composure, 'Ok mate - very funny. Maybe you should just fuck off now ok? You can take the piss out of how I look all you like - I've heard it all before. You're twisted mate - leave me the fuck alone or I'll -'

'Point taken friend. But I am not ridiculing you or laughing at your expense. I'll leave you now. But the offer stands'. The stranger walked away - back the way he came.

That was so fucked-up, thought Nigel.

Later that night - Nigel was shaving. In the mirror he stared, longer than usual. He hadn't examined his face this intensely since he was a child. He looked at all of his perceived flaws and then turned away in disgust every time he spotted another. 'That weirdo was right though - I do wish I were better looking — fat fucking chance of that' he said to himself. Nigel, reached up to turn off the little light cord for the mirror's backlight, when he noticed something had changed. His face was, well, better! His nose, which was once fat and squashed, like a space hopper that was being sat on, was now small and pointed just the right amount. It was the perfect nose. His skin appeared smoother and the flap of skin which once hung over one of his eyes was now gone. When he showed his girlfriend she couldn't believe her luck. She was happy for him too. She had noticed something else, however. Nigel's penis was an inch shorter than it had been. When she plucked up the courage to mention it, Nigel admitted he'd noticed too, and he explained the attractive stranger had suggested sacrifices were part of the deal. Neither partner worried much, as Nigel had plenty of length to spare.

Nigel began to go out more and more — daring to visit late bars and clubs — something he'd never even dreamed of doing before. He didn't give two shits about fidelity - this was an opportunity he'd never had before and he believed the universe owed him. But it wasn't what he'd expected at all. He was getting rejected repeatedly; over and over again. He was looked at with disdain, just like before, and called a creep when he plucked up enough courage to speak to a girl. He heard the words 'as if' far too many times. Despite his improved appearance, he was still below average and he was overreaching — only approaching the best looking girls in the bars.

Back home, Nigel looked in the mirror again and wished he were better looking. His appearance changed yet again. His jaw reshaped — the bone itself was remodelling and his hair became thicker and more luxurious. The blue in his eyes became brighter. His skin became smoother and after a few seconds his whole face shape had changed. He looked much better. He checked in his pants and his penis had lost another inch. 'Shit!' Nigel blurted. He'd forgotten about the dick thing.

Weeks went by and Nigel had drifted away from Tara. She still shared his bed but he wasn't interested in physical contact — and some nights he wouldn't even come home. He'd told Tara she wasn't attractive to him and that now he was attractive and normal, they weren't really suitable together. He even started talking about leagues - he was in the premier league and she was Sunday league 5-a-side, an analogy that left Tara crying all night long. But Nigel still wasn't successful with the best looking girls. He was able to go out on the pull - but still limited by this imaginary league he'd decided he was in. Some mediocre league - definitely not the premiership he'd bragged about to Tara. The top league women were rude to him. They were dismissive and unnecessarily cruel. 'I *will* be desirable to them,' he thought, 'I'll be a solid ten!'

One night, in a club, Nigel was rejected again. He went to the bathroom and looked into the mirror, 'I wish I were better looking!'. Nigel immediately changed. He was now good looking. He knew it. But was it enough? He wanted to be irresistible. He looked into the mirror yet again and said the words again, 'I wish I were better looking!'. Nigel was almost in love with himself at this point — but was it enough for the girls in the club — the instagram models? He said it again, 'I wish I were better looking!' And again. And again.

Numerous groups of men and women threw their shapes on the dance floor whilst many simply watched on the sidelines. Like a domino effect, one by one, the young beautiful people turned their gazes towards the toilet door, out of which Nigel had just stepped. He was unrecognisable to himself and would be to anyone who knew him. He stepped forward and headed to the bar. He was served a glass of champagne immediately, and a dozen women approached — barging each other and vying for his attention Nigel had done it — he was desirable. He was instagram-model-level attractive - Hollywood actor level hot — even hotter than that even! He exceeded the 'out of ten' scale of attractiveness. Tens looked like roadkill compared to him.

Nigel left the club that night with not one, not two, but three women. He not only had the looks but now also the confidence to live out his fantasies. He couldn't go back to Tara's house as she probably wouldn't approve of him cheating on her so blatantly, plus her appearance might put them all off. He'd be breaking up with her tomorrow anyway. Nigel found himself in one of the women's house; in her bedroom. All three women took turns kissing him passionately. He undressed them and kissed their bodies. They undressed him down to his underwear. They kissed each other then returned their attention back to him. They massaged oils into their skin, touched each other for Nigel's pleasure, and pushed him onto the bed, each girl licking a different body part. One woman couldn't wait any longer and removed Nigel's underwear with her teeth. Any other time this would have been erotic and exciting, but all three women stepped back and gasped. There was a scrotum, but no penis. They looked closer and closer, until they saw the little head of Nigel's penis — about half the size of a button mushroom, struggling to poke through the skin. Nigel felt erect too — so this was him at his best! 'Oh my God where is your dick — what the fuck!' said one of the girls loudly; horrified. Quickly this horror turned to disappointment, then amusement. They all laughed - the noise painfully wounded Nigel who fled to the bathroom and hid.

When Nigel returned to the bedroom to find his clothes and dress himself, carefully concealing his shame, the women asked him to leave. Nigel insisted this wasn't him — this was not his penis and something was wrong. He tried to convince the girls by describing the big manhood he remembered having, and he must have drunk too much that's all. Nigel was embarrassed, humiliated, and distraught. He heard them laughing as he left the house.

He got home and went straight to the bathroom. 'I wish my dick was big again'. The oddest sensation filled his groin — tingling and warmth. He could feel it growing and growing. He shouted, 'Yes! Yes, thank God!' Before pulling down his pants and checking himself out. He smiled and thanked god a few more times before looking up to the mirror. 'Oh God no' exclaimed Nigel. Nigel's face was as it was before; before the wishes. He was ugly Nigel again. He sobbed for a while before thinking, 'I can wish this all right! I can ask for both things — a big dick and a gorgeous face. I could just wish for attractiveness in every possible way'. He looked into the mirror and said, 'I wish to be attractive in every possible way'. The handsome stranger he'd met at the crossing days earlier, appeared in the mirror, startling Nigel who stepped back away from the mirror, only stopping because of the door behind him.

'I'm sorry, you have used up all of your wishes. Thank you for your time — and as a valued customer, I'd like to wish you a long and happy life. Please use code, 'wishwaste10' at any online beauty store for 10% off all beauty products. Goodbye'. The man showed no emotion and sounded like a recording. He disappeared and Nigel was left looking at his own reflection. He grabbed the nearest thing — the glass his toothbrush was in, and hurled it at his reflection. He rushed into the bedroom sobbing, 'Tara! Tara! It's gone — it's all gone! Baby please I need you!'. Nigel switched the light on and looked at the empty bed, then at the open, empty wardrobe, and then the open, empty drawers. A folded note on the bedside table was all that was left. He opened it:

I'm staying at my sister's place tonight. I want you out by the time I get back tomorrow afternoon. If you're still there when I return, I'll cut your dick off - if you still have one!

Nigel sobbed.

The Pervy Fly

16

A housefly buzzed around the bedroom and landed on the lampshade. A woman lying in bed wafted it away before continuing to kiss the man next to her. They removed each other's clothes and their bodies united. The fly landed on the curtain.

The sexual partners manoeuvred their bodies into various positions. They groaned and moaned, swore and whispered, and their hot sweaty bodies intertwined.

He penetrated her — and she moved her hips up and down rapidly from above — she bounced up and down on him like she was twerking on a space hopper. They both cried out in ecstasy — juices flowed and bodily fluids were exchanged. After two hours of sexual stimulation and the final climax — the pair rolled back and caught their breaths. They lit up cigarettes and smiled.

The fly finished his wank, and wiped his aedeagus - it's a kind of insect dick - on the curtains, before flying towards the slightly open window, 'Phwoar,' thought the fly, 'that was hot! Now for Fiona and Mike at number 23 - they should be going at it in a few minutes - I should be able to go feast on some dog shit on the way, if I don't mind missing the foreplay'.

The woman looked over at her partner with a puzzled look, 'Did you see that fly watching us?' she asked.
   'Yeah. Fucking pervert! I think I heard him say he was off to number 23 next' said the man.

'Yeah. I'd better call Fiona and tell her to close her windows' said the woman, reaching over for the telephone. 'Hi Fiona, it's Jane. Yeah good thanks. Listen, just to let you know, that bloody fly's back. Yeah, yeah shut the windows. I'll call the police but I doubt they'll come out until morning. Ok love, have fun. Don't forget the curtains' Jane laughed. 'Yeah. See you soon. Traa love. Bye..bye..' Jane hung up the phone.

'I told her but I reckon that dirty bitch loves being watched' Jane said with in a judgemental tone.

'I wouldn't put it past her — she's into all-sorts I heard. Perverts! How about round two sexy? I'll get the whip and nipple clamps — you grab the jump leads' he said.

The Lying Fly

17

There once was a fly. This fly was the leader of the flies. One day at a fly meeting, a few of the flies expressed their concern about sticky, invisible traps scattered throughout the town that flies were getting trapped in and eaten by monsters that lurked in the shadows. The fly leader assured the community there were no such things as monsters or invisible traps. Some flies insisted they'd seen other flies trapped mid-air, some flies insisted they'd barely escaped with their lives, and the rest of the flies, the majority, laughed at the ludicrous claims, and carried on business as usual, landing on dog shit immediately followed by landing on some poor unsuspecting human's food. That was their primary job — everything else was secondary.

Time passed, and more and more flies became worried about the monsters and their invisible traps. 'there's no such thing. This is fear-mongering and completely unfounded!' said the leader.

More time passed, and another meeting was held. This time, all of the flies said they'd seen their kin trapped in the sky, and an 8-legged monster with many eyes and hairy skin, devour their friends and family. The leader still insisted there was nothing to worry about and that monsters weren't real — stating this was all just 'fake news'.

Another meeting was held. This time, the flies did not speak up about the climate of fear — as the leader brought up the issue himself, 'Friends - some of my top advisors have found that there are indeed silky sneaky snares out there — but I assure you there is nothing to worry about. There are no monsters and this will all pass. As you know, I am very old, some 19 days old, and I beseech you to heed my wisdom. Relax, and I hope you all have a truly shitty weekend'.

Two days later, another meeting was held. Far fewer flies attended for they had either died from old age, or from being caught by the monsters. The leader spoke, 'My friends, the floating snares are clearly very real, as I've always said. I urge all of you to stay alert, and stay at home, unless you need to lay eggs or land on shit and human food. If you are caught in a snare, stay where you are and wait for help'. The fly community were confused by this response — but decided to trust their leader.

More flies died and another meeting was held. 'My friends, our first point of business is to pay tribute to Harold, who bravely flew into the mouth of a cyclist and was never seen again. A true fly hero. Sources suggest that he had just been rolling around in dog shit prior to the swallowing — so he did not die in vain. He was truly dedicated to the cause. It was a noble death; a hero's death. Our next point of business, is the snares and so-called monsters terrorising our town. To put your minds to rest - I will accompany you on a trip to some of the areas said to host these monsters. Joyce, has informed us that Dave has been caught in a trap and needs assistance. Thank you Joyce for the information. If we can all follow Joyce please, she'll lead the way'.

So all the flies followed Joyce, and lo-and-behold, there was Dave, wriggling around in mid-air.

'Dave! Oiy Dave! What's going on?' Shouted the leader.

'I'm bloody trapped in something. I can't see it but it's there! There's a bloody monster just staring at me in the corner! Help me for God's sake!'

'Dave you're perfectly fine. Everybody, I'll show you just how safe it is in the snare' said the leader.

So the leader flew over to Dave, and as you'd expect, became trapped. He shouted to his fly community not to worry and that everything was fine.

At that very moment, something appeared from the shadows in the corner of the silky snare. It was the monster. But the leader did not panic. 'Hello, there. I'm the leader of the flies. Who might you be?'

'I'm a spider, mate. I don't usually chat to my food, but whatever'.

'Oh jolly good. So what is it that you do? And would you be a dear old sport, and help me and Dave out of whatever this is?'

'It's a web. It's my web. And no, I'm hungry. I'm going to eat you. First I'll paralyse you with a bite, and then wrap you up in my silk, then devour you when I'm good and ready. I'll be honest, it's not going to be pleasant for either of you'

'Oh shit!' said Dave.

'Oh dear' said the leader.

The rest of the flies fled in terror. The spider did what he'd promised, whilst wondering how the hell such an imbecilic fool became their leader, and why his food tasted of shit.

The flies got home and voted for another leader who promised not to make the same mistakes of the past. But the flies kept flying into the spider's web — because they're flies and it's what they do — secondary to landing on human food whilst covered in dog-shit.

18

After 17 failed attempts, Professor Beru flipped a switch on a control panel, lifted the crucifix around her neck to her lips and kissed it, then slammed her palm down onto a big red button, '18th time lucky!' she whispered, unconvincingly.

A siren sounded, and a flashing red light filled the lab. Steam blasted from the rim of a huge fluid-filled cylindrical glass pod in front of her. Massive tubes extended from the pod into the ceiling, popping and dropping away, one by one. The lid of the pod separated from it, pulled up by a mechanical arm. More steam rose from the glass chamber, and the fluid drained away, revealing an exact replica of herself.

Professor Beru leaned into a microphone extending from the control panel, 'Hello. Your designation is 18. My name is Professor Beru, your creator. You should have received full neuro-programming and understand my words. Tell me how you are feeling please'.

'Confused. Hungry. Where am I?' Came the reply.

'You're in my lab. You're a clone. I've cloned you. It's taken over a decade and many, many failures, but I've finally done it. You're a success!'

'Why have you created me?' The clone asked.

'To do my job, my life admin, and my chores. Oh and sleep with my husband — he's gotten old and fat and I can't stand him touching me'. The professor shuddered.

'Accessing transferred memories' the clone spoke like a robot. 'Accessing, Mr Alan Beru'. The clone stared vacantly ahead for a moment, before looking over to the Professor and speaking harshly, 'Eew God no — fuck your own minging husband — eew gross'. The clone grabbed her own head, right hand under the chin, left hand on the left side of her head, and with one mighty push, snapped her own neck and fell to the floor.

'Aww shit. Another failure' muttered Professor Beru, lowering her head in despair.

Rover

19

Rover didn't give a shit. He got up when he wanted, slept when he wanted, and ate when he wanted. He even shat when and where he wanted; often choosing Mrs Shelton's front lawn, which he was fond of.

Recently Rover had taken to dragging his arse across the carpet. It itched so much. It turned out he had worms and had to take some pills with his food to get rid of them.

He'd go for walks 3 times a day for exercise, but he was getting on a bit and he didn't like to be away from home for too long. There was a border collie at number 13 across the road, and if Rover saw her, he'd run over and take a good deep sniff of her arse. Much to the distress of the owner Mrs Beckles, whose leg Rover would hump.

Rover was arrested on 9 July 2019 for indecent exposure, public indecency, sexual assault and harassment. Rover wasn't his first name — it was his last. His first name was Roy, but everybody called him Rover because he acted a bit like a dog

Mrs Beckles from number 13 was said to have suffered great distress from Roy's behaviour and was being treated for depression, PTSD, and social anxiety. Her border collie was being treated for the same.

Roy was committed to a mental health institute for psychiatric assessment and rehabilitation. The rehabilitation was a failure and unfortunately, later that year, Roy had to be put down.

Future Theatre

20

Quite a long time ago, a young man by the name of Guido, had a theory that time travel was not only possible, but time travellers from the future were already visiting the past.

Guido had researched thousands upon thousands of portraits across the centuries and correlated them with written descriptions of the individuals at the time, and found that a small percentage of these portraits resembled portraits that had preceded them centuries prior. This recurred throughout history, and at times of culturally or historically significant events, the same faces appeared in contemporary art of the time. They'd pop up time and time again, usually in the background doing something innocuous. One face in particular, which was very distinctive, recurred throughout history at pivotal moments, along with historical accounts that described him in great detail — and with great consistency. He was the same person, spanning hundreds of years, and he had no qualms in being seen. He even went to the extent of becoming involved in significant events and was well known amongst significant people of the time, fraternising with the monarchies, politicians, and artists of the day — hence the detailed descriptions existing in scrolls, diaries, literature, transcripts, journals, and eventually newspapers.

Guido had to know who this man was — and prove his theory. So after some careful planning, Guido set a trap. He would become involved in as many significant events as he could — travelling throughout the continent, involving himself in wars and plots and anything in-between, all in the hope that his time travelling intruder would reveal himself.

Years passed and Guido had no success. Something had to be done. An opportunity presented itself. Guido met the perfect crowd for a revolution.

Guido and his pals had decided to overthrow the king of England and destroy the parliament house with Gunpowder. This would certainly attract time travelling historians of the future.

So the explosives were in place and Guido was left to guard the gunpowder. He waited and waited until a figure approached from the shadows, holding what looked like a lamp but Guido couldn't help but notice it didn't flicker and no flame was visible — it was like the torch was harnessing sunlight itself, redirecting it; focussing it and beaming it into his eyes, blinding his vision momentarily.

The man introduced himself and said he was pleased to meet Guido. He even took a selfie with him, although Guido had no idea what a selfie was. Guido explained how he'd orchestrated this meeting, and that he had many questions. The time traveller seemed impressed. Guido explained that he had no intention of blowing anything up — but his actual plan had been successful. The man explained that his plan had been successful too. He'd intended to meet Guido and Guido had intended to meet him. That's a success story.

They asked each other questions and were blown away by the answers. The travelling man asked many more questions and seemed more curious than Guido was. After his curiosity was satisfied, Guido took the opportunity to take over the questioning. The man offered Guido the chance to ask about the past or the future, and he would show him whatever he wished, removing a device from his knapsack and placing it on the ground. Guido asked what it was. 'You'll see' came the reply.

Guido was offered five minutes to ask whatever he wanted. So he wasted no time at all in getting started.

Firstly, Guido asked about war. The man typed into his handheld device and the device on the ground projected a light directly at Guido's forehead. His jaw dropped and his eyes widened. The time traveller was projecting recorded history directly into Guido's mind. Guido learned about the Thirty Years' War, The English Civil Wars, The Seven Years' War, the numerous revolutions across the globe, the Napoleonic Wars, the American Civil War, World War One and it's sequel World War Two, The Korean War, The Vietnam War, The Iraq War, The Afghanistan War, World War Three, and the AI Wars, to name but a handful.

Guido was blown away. The light beaming into his little brain ceased. Guido couldn't believe the destruction and death. He couldn't believe the weaponry and advances in warfare. He couldn't believe how the world hadn't learned from history.

'You have four minutes remaining,' said the time traveller.

'What? I got all that knowledge in the space of one minute? This technology is surely witchcraft!' said Guido, who'd never used the word technology before, as he'd only just learned it from his history lesson.

Guido chose more generally for his next lesson. He asked to see what life would look like over the next two hundred years. Once again the light beamed through Guido's thick skull and into his brain.

'Wow! So many inventions! So many achievements!' Guido exclaimed, 'Show me more!'

Guido used his remaining minutes having all of history beamed into his brain, right the way up until the time traveller's own time.

At one point, Guido pulled away from the light, looking concerned. He claimed to see empty streets and roads, people locked away in their homes and avoiding each other. The only ones who were outside, wore masks. There were protests and violence, oppressive states, and so much death. And why were people wearing face masks?

'That's 2020' said the time traveller, 'Don't ask'.

The light resumed and Guido's eyes widened further still. His time was up and the light ceased. Guido was drooling a little from having his mouth wide open for the past 5 minutes.

The time traveller explained it was time to leave. He picked up his device and returned it to his bag.

'I'll walk out of the cave with you' said Guido.

Suddenly, some voices could be heard approaching.

'Quick, we need to hide' said Guido in a low voice.

'There's nowhere to hide' replied the man.

'What shall we do?' Guido asked.

'Well, I'm off back to my own time my friend. And you are about to be arrested' said the man in a very matter of fact monotone.

'What? You can't leave me here!' Guido cried.

'Oh Guy, I'm the one who told them you were here' came the traveller's reply.

'Why would you do that?' said a shocked Guido.

'Because it's what happened here. I read all about it. You get arrested and you'll be executed,' came the cold reply.

'Oh my Lord'. Guido's voice trembled, 'please, you have to help me?'

'Fine' the man replied.

'Oh thank you! Thank you so much' said Guido.

'Here's some advice: when they try to hang you, just jump from the scaffolding before they get the chance. It'll save you a lot of pain and suffering. Right, must be off. It was fascinating meeting you, Mr Fawkes. Don't let the torture get you down too much eh,' said the man, tapping his handheld device.

But Guido had learned all about the technology the time traveller was using - a fortunate knowledge bi-product of the history lesson. Before the traveller could vanish into thin air, Guido kicked him in his nuts and shouted, 'Yoink!', snatching the device from the time traveller's hands and disappearing in a flash of light forever, to where, we do not know.

'Oh shit,' said the time traveller.

How are you?

21

Phil walked along the long corridor at work that lead to the staffroom. The guy from sales he liked was walking towards him. Phil's heart rate increased and butterflies were fucking around in his belly like they fucking owned the place.

The guy approached closer and closer until they were within talking distance and making eye-contact. They didn't know each other well enough to stop and talk, so it would be a quick nod and a 'how ya doin?' and then everyone could continue with their lives as if it had no bearing on the universe at all. Phil couldn't remember if his name was Adam, or Alan. Or was it Arthur? Did it even begin with an 'A'? Too late to use his name now, so it'd have to be 'mate' or 'pal' or something. *No, not pal, that's ridiculous, don't be an idiot! So lame.*

Here it was, the moment he'd anticipated for literally seconds.

The nod came from Adam, Alan, or Arthur. It was Phil's moment, and he took it.

'Hey, how are you?' Phil asked.
'Not bad thanks, you?' Enquired Adam, Alan, or Arthur.
'Yeah good thanks, you?' Phil replied.
'Erm, yeah, still good..thanks' came the reply.

Adam, Alan or Arthur looked at Phil a little bemused and kept walking. Phil wanted the ground to open up and swallow him whole. *I wish I was dead,* he thought, over and over again. And he did die - on the inside.

Phil dwelled on that moment for the rest of his life. He barely spoke a word to anybody else after that day. And about sixty years later, he died alone - still thinking of that awkward moment in his twenties. Some say that Phil finally died of embarrassment.

First time, last time

22

Kieran met Dan in the only gay club in the City. He wasn't out to his family yet so he couldn't bring him home, plus how lame is it to still live with your parents when you're twenty-one. Kieran suggested going back to Dan's house. Dan was about six or seven years older than Kieran, and so this wasn't anything new — he wasn't nervous at all. Kieran however, hadn't been with anyone before. He was confident, but nervous. They hit it off and the chemistry was instantaneous. They had shared experiences, had common interests, loved the same food, holiday destinations, and tv shows, and they were both intelligent and funny. Perfect for each other. What a connection!

At Dan's house, they tore each others clothes off and kissed passionately. Dan pushed Kieran onto his back and pulled his boxers down past his ankles and tossed them onto the bedroom floor. Then he paused.

'What is it?' Asked Kieran, perplexed.

'Oh nothing — it's fine' replied Dan before continuing the kissing and caressing.

Dan then stopped.

'Why did you look at my dick and pause?' Asked Kieran.

'No reason'

'Well it must be for some reason'

'Well, it's just my last boyfriend was big in the downstairs department so to speak. I suppose I'd become accustomed to it'. Dan explained.

'So what am I? Small?' Asked Kieran with some hostility.

'No! No! I mean, you're average. It's fine' said Dan.

'Ok. Fine. I'm happy with that. I'm not upset at all because average is just another way of saying 'normal' which I'm ok with. So I'm just like most people. I'll take that. At least you didn't say mediocre! Jeez. Mediocre is much worse - like worse than average. It's like saying, it's less than average - unimpressive. Rubbish basically', Kieran was rambling at this point and his erection had long since left the building.

'Yeah that's the word I was looking for! Mediocre - it's mediocre! Mediocre at best. That's what I meant. Much better word' said Dan as if remembering the answer to a question on a game show.

Kieran got dressed and left.

Kieran spent the next sixty years investing his time and resources in penis enlargement.

On his deathbed, he looked down at his mediocre penis, and realised he should have maybe invested his time in some other things. The hospice nurse looked bewildered and put a sheet over his penis as if covering a dead body. Something she'd do again to his actual dead body later that day.

Dan spent the rest of his days in search of someone with as big a penis as his ex-boyfriend's. He never found what he was looking for, and on his deathbed, thought about that guy he met that time, the one with the mediocre penis, and thought that maybe he should have pursued things with him, because he'd never met anyone more perfect and alike. If it wasn't for his penis obsession — he could have been very happy.

Such a pair of dicks.

What's your name again?

23

You know when somebody at work knows your name but you don't know theirs? And you wonder how long they've known yours and how long you've not known theirs? Doug was one of those people. Every day without fail, the woman in the same block of flats said, 'hello' or 'good morning,' as it was usually in the morning as they were both heading off to work. Except, she wouldn't just say, 'good morning' or 'hello,' it would be 'good morning, Doug,' or 'Hello, Doug'. Doug had a number of options at this point: he could say, 'Hello' or 'good morning' back, or throw in a 'dear' or 'love' at the end. But he was too young for that, it didn't sound or feel right coming from his lips. The other option, which was't really an option at all, was to ask her name. But how could he? It must have been months since he first encountered her — and NOW he asks her name! How rude would he look? Maybe it hadn't been months — maybe it'd been years. Maybe they used to work together or something? Or even further back, went to school or college together? Oh my lord — what if they'd slept together? You see, Doug was trapped. He couldn't ask her name now, he'd left it too long. But likewise, he couldn't go on saying hello back, without using her name — eventually she'd grow suspicious. He dreaded the day when she would inevitably confront him, 'What is my name?' she'd ask. Doug would wish for death at that moment and hope it was swift. Doug was just too polite to upset or offend anyone; not a bad character trait, but not a flawless one either.

This didn't *only* happen with the woman in his building, this had happened to Doug a number of times. Doug used to walk a much quicker route to work in a morning, but this guy used to walk the same way, and he'd pass Doug, but he'd pass him so slowly, because his pace was only marginally faster than Doug's, it made it a very uncomfortable few seconds, that felt like minutes. This guy would shout, unnecessarily, 'alright Dougie' and Doug would reply, 'Hey man! How ya'doin?' Doug had no idea who this man was, and took the decision to change his route into work; the longer, less scenic route — all because he didn't have the courage to ask someone's name.

One morning, Doug stepped out of his flat and into the corridor. He checked the door was locked by giving it a good yank a couple of times, then popped his keys in his pocket and walked to the stairwell. There he saw the woman. She smiled and he smiled back. Doug thought he'd gotten away with just a look — he wouldn't have to talk, which could leave him vulnerable to getting found out for the fraudster he was. But he hadn't gotten away with it, instead, the woman manoeuvred herself between Doug and the stairs. *Oh God*, he thought. Will she want an actual conversation this time? What if his secret is exposed? She'll be so offended. She'll tell everybody in the building. He'll be a pariah of civility and have to leave the flats and move away to another city.

As Doug panicked, the woman talked. Doug wasn't taking anything in, he was too busy thinking about how horrible this situation was and how he should get out of it. But it looked like he had gotten out of it, because she'd stopped talking and was now looking at him blankly. Maybe that was it? He just had to say 'great, good to see you, catch you later' or something ambiguous to move on. So he did just that. Except things didn't move on. She replied, but not with a 'see you' or 'bye' or anything like that. No, she replied with, 'great! I'll give you my number!' What the hell had he agreed to? Oh shit! Shit shit shit! She got her phone out of her handbag, and he did the same. She asked if he was ready, and Doug replied in the affirmative. But he wasn't ready. The first bit of adding a new contact on a mobile phone, is the bit that asks for the contacts name - quite an important bit. Doug panicked and typed in *'Apartment woman'*; now he was ready. She read her number out in that annoying, slow, one digit at a time kind of way that takes ages and is just plain irritating. He took down the number and hit save. 'Let me take a look and see if you've taken it down right' she said. *Oh God!* Doug panicked. She'd see that he'd put her down as *'building woman'* and all would be exposed. He pulled his phone back defensively, which took her a little by surprise. 'It's ok - I'll just drop call you it's easier' he said. And so he drop called her. Was that the end of it? Would this nightmare ever end? Nope. She turned and walked away from Doug, down the stairs and opened the main door to the building, and turned, 'Great, Doug - I'll see you this evening then? You can come over about seven o'clock. Can't wait!'

Doug was mortified. It seems he'd agreed to go on a date with a women whose name he didn't know. Or was it a date? He could have agreed to helping her put shelves up. No, that was sexist, why would she need help with that? She'd probably be better at it than he was. What else could it be? Maybe she wants a coffee? Or maybe he's agreed to look after her cat or something. Maybe she's going on a date and she needed him to watch her dog. Oh god please be something else — anything other than the date. Normally he'd be flattered, but the awkwardness was unbearable and he already had a girlfriend. But he'd agreed to something.

Doug decided he'd go over — prepared for any scenario. He'd wear smart casual — an outfit for any occasion, including pet-sitting and dating.

It did turn out to be a date, and Doug felt uncomfortable all evening. Doug and the woman dated for 6 months. During that time, he never caught her name. He met her friends and her parents, and her work colleagues; something he looked forward to because they'd inevitably use her name at some point — but no. He couldn't believe it! Nobody used her name! Maybe they were all like him - they'd become trapped in her life the same way he had - not knowing her name and agreeing to stuff they didn't mean to. *But that can't be it, I'm sure her parents know her name. I hope so anyway,* thought Doug. Doug was already starting to feel like his life was falling apart, when she asked him to move in with her. His actual girlfriend had dumped him because he was never available, due to the inadvertent dates he was going on with 'Apartment woman'; his now girlfriend. Doug didn't want to be rude, he'd already done enough damage by not knowing his now girlfriend's name, he couldn't make things worse by saying no to this. So he said yes. He also saw an opportunity; her post would have her name on. He could check out her name on her letters! *Thank you Royal Mail!*

As it turned out, his inadvertent girlfriend was passionate about the environment and made sure all of her correspondence was paperless - she received it all by email. Email! He'd ask for her email address - to send some funny gifs or memes or some shite like that. Her e-mail address was 'EarthGirlStar9243@' something or other. Damn it! He tried and tried to get her name - you name it - he tried it.

Then came their wedding day. Doug was about to marry a woman whose name he did not know. His friends and family would be there - and rather than admit to them that he didn't know her name, he'd given her the pet name Poppy, because she liked poppies and he thought he could get away with giving her that as a cute pet name. So his fiancee would hopefully say her own name during the ceremony, you know the bit where they say, 'I Joe Bloggs, take thee Sally Smith, to be your lawful blah blah blah'. He would therefore learn her name for the first time and his problem would be solved. He'd then have to explain to everyone that Poppy was just a nickname.

The moment came. She said the words, 'I, Karen Smith, take you, Doug Ballinger, to be your…'

Karen! KAREN! Fucking Karen! That was it? That's what he'd been waiting for? Doug was disappointed to say the least, he'd waited so long for a name — and it turned out to be such a plain name. No offence if you're a Karen, but it is plain, like most names. He wasn't just disappointed, he was angry. He wanted to shout out at the top of his lungs, 'Oh fuck you, Karen!' But he didn't — because it was their wedding day.

Doug went on to have three children with Karen. They were very rude children who said whatever the fuck they wanted, whenever the fuck they wanted. Doug liked and encouraged this. Doug was so proud because he knew they'd never end up getting married and having children with someone out of politeness or embarrassment as he had done - they were too rude and inconsiderate for that. He loved those kids. He never caught their names though.

Role Play

WARNING - THIS CHAPTER CONTAINS BAD LANGUAGE, SCENES OF A GRAPHIC AND SEXUAL NATURE AND REFERENCES TO RAPE - PLEASE CONTINUE WITH CAUTION. YOU'LL BE OFFENDED. SERIOUSLY - JUST SKIP IT

24

....

Some people are into some weird shit. Most people have something they're into that deviates from the norm, something taboo or kinky. Everybody has a thing.

Barry's thing was role play. Not any old role play - but very aggressive S&M role play. Specifically, Barry liked to pretend that he was being attacked and forced into sexual servitude. He liked to be whipped, slapped, spat on and degraded in ways you couldn't imagine. He loved to be spanked. He loved to be tied-up, blindfolded, and gagged. He particularly enjoyed the apprehension building up to the finale. The adrenaline rush was mind-blowing. The finale always involved a lot of lubrication and a very large dildo. Don't judge.

Barry didn't care who carried out the fantasy — gender wasn't important — it was all about the domination and humiliation. Barry had a high powered job you see, and after spending all day telling other people what to do, he liked to let all of that go and allow himself to be dominated.

On this occasion, Barry had been on a website that caters to his specific needs and arranged for a couple of chaps to come over that night, break in, and have their wicked way with him in his own bedroom. I say break in; actually, the key was left under the pot plant near the doorstep for his assailants to help themselves to, as per their agreement. Barry had asked his guests to arrive as late as possible — he preferred it when they turned up after he'd fallen asleep, which wasn't always possible, as Barry was often too excited to sleep.

So Barry waited in bed — trying to force his brain to be quiet, but it was in vain; his mind was racing and his excitement got the better of him. It was now midnight and nobody had arrived. The later it got, the more excited he got. Barry was aroused in anticipation. He couldn't wait for the first sign of intruders. It would be a noise — the door being opened — or footsteps coming up his creaky stairs. Those sounds always gave him butterflies and a warm funny feeling down below. So Barry waited. And waited. And waited some more.

But nobody came. It was now 4am and Barry's excitement had dwindled somewhat. He turned his bedside lamp on and reached for his laptop, opening the lid and tapping the keys in frustration. He was messaging the two members of the website who he'd paid good money to to give him a good seeing to. They weren't showing as being online — and there was no number to call them on. So he sent them an angry message on the website, and slammed his laptop shut. He'd stayed awake all night — for nothing. At least tomorrow, or today even, as it was now the early hours, he wasn't at work and could catch up on missed sleep — for it was Saturday.

Since Barry's excitement had dissipated — he was now able to fall asleep. No sooner had his heavy eyes shut than a high-pitched wailing siren filled the room, startling Barry, who sat bolt-upright at the noise; it was deafening, and was now accompanied by blue flashing lights penetrating his curtains and illuminating his bedroom like a nightclub. Barry recognised the siren, 'WOOOOOOOooo wooooooooooo. WOOOOOOOO wooooooo'. It was a police siren. But what were they doing on his street? Then another siren came, 'WOOoo Wa Wu Wa Wu Wa Wu Wa'. It must have been an ambulance. What the hell is happening out there? The noise stopped but the light continued to fill Barry's bedroom. 'For God's sake - can I not get an ounce of sleep tonight?' Barry said to himself.

Eventually, everything returned to normal and Barry finally drifted off to sleep.

Barry woke about midday. He really needed the lie in. After his late breakfast and a shower, Barry made himself his second cup of tea of the day. He decided to take himself and his tea into the garden, as it was a nice hot day. He sat on one of the patio chairs and sipped his tea.

'Psssst. Pssst. Barry?' The irritating noise persisted, 'Pssst. Pssst'

Barry thought the noise was annoying but his annoyance was superseded by his curiosity as to why his neighbour was climbing over their dividing garden fence.

'Ted?' Barry responded.

'Did you hear? Ted asked excitedly.

'Hear what?' Barry replied.

'What happened last night? You must have heard all the commotion?' said Ted.

'Yeah - kept me awake half the night. Go on then - I can see you're itching to tell me' said Barry, patronisingly. Ted had managed to get over the fence by now and was now stood over Barry.

'It's Mr Edmonton at number 2. He was attacked last night!' Ted was out of breath from the fence and had to pause.

'What? What do you mean attacked? At home? Come on man speak up,' demanded Barry, already making connections that filled him with dread.

'Some men broke in to his house. Apparently he keeps a spare key under his pot plant and they must have been watching him beforehand because they knew to look under it. They let themselves in and they — oh my god - I can't even say it' Ted put his hand to his mouth as if stopping himself from being sick. Barry had changed colour; a kind of pale he'd never turned before. The awful realisation had hit him in the belly hard.

'What? What did they do?' begged Barry, overwhelmed by guilt.

'They did perverse things to him! They even used nipple clamps. They even brought their own gear! How sick is that?'

'Oh my God! Is he ok?' asked Barry, with trepidation.

'He's in hospital but he's stable' Ted replied, reassuringly.

'Oh! Thank God! Erm, I've got to go,' insisted Barry, rather abruptly.

Barry rushed off into the house leaving Ted confused and alone in the garden. Barry went straight to his computer and checked the original message he'd sent yesterday with his contact details:

"Hey you bad men — still on for later? Key will be under the pot plant. It's Fountain Street, number 2"

'Oh shit!' Barry's eyes widened - awful realisation took hold.

Barry was number 22 Fountain Street. Not number 2. He'd fucked up - big time. How do you miss a '2'? Maybe the key got stuck or something? Maybe he tapped too lightly? *Fucking keyboard!*

'Poor old Mr Edmonton - he'd been in a world war for God's sake! He was a hero! How could I do such a thing?' Barry sobbed.

A new unread message popped up on his screen. It was from the two men:

'Hey. Hope you got what you needed from last night. Payment received - thanks. But listen, we can't come over and do that again - you're way too good at role play - it all got a bit too real for our tastes - you should have got an Oscar for your performance! Amazed and impressed you resisted using the safe word! You've got some balls man. Anyway, sorry we couldn't retrieve that toy - it did seem to get stuck good and proper - but that's ok - you can keep it. Happy hunting ya crazy bitch'

Barry placed his face into his hands, and sobbed again. 'Oh God no!' he cried.

Moral of the story: fetishes have consequences. Or is it, pay more attention to detail? Always proof-read emails? One of those.

The Superhero

25

The world had mixed feelings about Donnie Driftwood; a mild-mannered postman by day; a high-powered superhero by night..and day if the situation required it, superseding his postal duties. Actually, nothing much happened at night, plus Donnie didn't like being out when it got dark — all those unsavoury characters, and foxes..he was scared of foxes.

All Superheroes have an origin story right? Correct. And Donnie is no different. When Donnie was a teenager, a magnificent wizard appeared with a dazzling aura glowing so bright that Donnie had to ask him if he could turn down the brightness a bit, which he did obligingly with an apology on top. The wizard told Donnie he had heard his prayers. Donnie didn't realise wizards heard prayers but apparently they do. Donnie was beaten up at school and wished he had the power to annihilate his bullies. He'd imagined making them burst into flames with his mind — but decided it was a bad idea because he didn't need superpowers for that, just a can of petrol and some matches. He then went home, got on his knees, rested his elbows on his bed, and placed his palms together and turned his wish into a prayer. Donnie opened his eyes and the wizard was stood there before him. At first Donnie assumed a neighbourhood peadophile had climbed up the drainpipe and through the window. Once the wizard had begged Donnie not to call the police and convinced him he was a wizard, not a paedo, the conversation could advance past such awkward misunderstandings. It took a few magic tricks to convince Donnie, but it was worth it - the wizard couldn't face more jail time; his bail conditions were very clear. So the wizard got to the point, saying he would grant Donnie's wish to become a powerful superhero. But so that Donnie wouldn't abuse his power, and only use it when absolutely necessary, it had one caveat. In order to activate his powers, Donnie had to eat a baby. Donnie couldn't believe his ears! He asked the wizard why he would add such a terrible condition to his wish, and made it clear that he would never be able to use his powers at such a cost! The wizard laughed, stating that the last thing he wanted was for Donnie to use his powers - otherwise he'd be murdering school bullies and decapitating people for littering, or making people explode for looking at him the wrong way. Donnie accepted this. He knew deep down that with great power came catastrophic vengeance and probably eventual genocide. Power corrupts. Plus, how do you devour a whole baby? Or do you have to eat it bit by bit? Maybe cooked into a casserole or something? Donnie thought about using his power for good, not vengeance. He could become a superhero and save lives. But then again, in the event of a sudden disaster or emergency, he wouldn't have time to bake a baby casserole, and lots of people would die because of his lengthy powering-up process. The wizard heard Donnie's thoughts and explained that he would have to devour the baby whole, and that he could do this like an anaconda swallowing its prey. The wizard did a wee spell that altered Donnie's anatomy to allow for such a feat, and then added the innate superpowers that Donnie vowed to never use, less he become a murderer of the worst kind. The wizard laughed again, then climbed out of the window and down the drainpipe before running off into the distance, nearly tripping over his own cloak. Donnie wondered why the wizard couldn't just make himself vanish but it wasn't important enough to dwell on. It's more of a mystery that the wizard went straight to an off-licence and began shoplifting cider. But that's another story for another time.

The world had other superheroes but none of them were as powerful as Donnie. It wasn't known whether the wizard was responsible for all such powers in the world, but Donnie knew he was the most powerful one of them all; he could feel it, even though he had never ever used his powers — the price was too high. None of the other heroes had to do anything heinous for their powers, which bothered Donnie a lot. But their superpowers were crap so he took some solace in that.

Now his teenage years were behind him, and he'd forgotten all about such childish things as superpowers and wizards. All he had to think about now was delivering the post and paying his bills. He had a girlfriend too, whom he loved dearly, and who was pregnant with his child. They were happy. Her name was Joan. I know, what a weirdly old-fashioned name for a young woman. Donnie had got over it so you should too.

One Saturday, Donnie and his girlfriend Joan, and her bump, were just leaving a Mother Care store on a busy high street. If this makes you anxious - owing to all the baby eating talk, don't worry, his girlfriend wasn't worried, and Donnie hadn't given it any thought since his teenage years. Plus, what emergency or disaster could possibly happen outside Mother Care on a Saturday afternoon? Nothing the emergency services couldn't handle. So don't worry.

So then a meteor appeared out of nowhere and hurtled towards Mother Care. Sorry, I know I said don't worry, but I didn't know a meteor would appear from space and threaten to wipe out the entire city and Mother Care with it. Everybody stared up in disbelief. Some legs turned to jelly, and some froze in terror. As the meteor got closer and closer, it cast a shadow over the people below. The darkness added to the fear and many people ran and screamed, shoving and trampling over each other; it was like Black Friday in a JD Sports. Some of the parents who'd left Mother Care were stood, frozen in fear, clutching their babies. Some crouched down, hugged and kissed their toddlers, knowing this was the end. Donnie looked into Joan's teary eyes and asked her a question. He asked her to forgive him. Joan didn't ask what she should forgive, but instead told him that he was scaring her.

'I'm sorry, I have to do this' said Donnie.

'Do what? Oh my God Donnie - we're going to die!' cried Joan, who collapsed to the floor, her trembling jelly legs unable to hold her upright any longer.

'I've got to go and do something awful now. It's the only way' said Donnie, who turned to walk away.

'Don't leave us! Donnie! Get back here now! Donnie! Donnie! Donnie!', Joan cried uncontrollably. Her cries were as audible as the screams and it was excruciating for Donnie to hear. He walked over to a trembling woman, who held tightly to her tiny baby. Donnie reached over to her, 'I can save you. I can save everyone'. Donnie must have come across as the messiah or something, because the mother released her hold of the infant. Donnie held the baby and took a step back. 'I'm so sorry. I'm so, so sorry love'. As Donnie said the words he felt tears streaming down his cheeks. The mother looked scared and confused. 'What for? What are you going to do? Give me back my baby!' The mother tried to snatch her baby back but Donnie pushed her to the ground and turned one-hundred and eighty degrees to face Joan. He couldn't do this in front of the baby's mother, so he turned to the mother of his unborn child. He didn't want her to see this either, but there was no time.

'What are you doing, Donnie? Give her her baby back!' Joan shouted at Donnie like a mother yelling at a child to return a snatched toy to its younger sibling.

'I'm sorry. I'm so sorry! Please forgive me!' Donnie looked into Joan's eyes as he begged for forgiveness, before turning his gaze to the infant. He looked into the infants eyes, who was oddly calm and seemed to have hiccups. Donnie cried. He begged the child for forgiveness too, before dislocating his own jaw and opening his mouth wider than humanly possible. He pushed the baby into his wide open mouth and gulped. The shape of the baby could be seen sliding down his gullet like some poor bunny devoured by a python. The baby was crying now, and it's muffled screams could be heard from inside Donnie. People screamed in horror and wept in grief. The mother wailed until she passed out. Joan fainted. But Donnie felt a power surge through his veins - a power like nothing he could have ever imagined. He felt the immense power and knew what he had to do - he knew the power wouldn't last long, and didn't fancy eating another baby for a top-up. No, he had to deal with this potential catastrophe straight away. He looked up at the meteor, bent his knees, and pushed himself with astonishing force into the air towards the meteor. Thrust created a sonic boom, and within seconds Donnie had smashed the meteor to pieces. The break-away smaller meteor fragments would cause wide spread devastation too, so he flew from one to the next, hurling them back into space. It all happened at such speed, nobody could follow what was happening with their limited human eyes. Donnie landed back outside Mother Care. His body emanated a glowing energy field not dissimilar to the wizards. It was a proper Superhero landing. He was buzzing. The sky was now clear and the crowds looked at Donnie in amazement. The mother who had fainted, and his wife who had done the same were now conscious and looking at Donnie. They were saved. Donnie had saved the day. He felt the powers disappear and the glowing energy dissipated. He was back to normal. The crowd booed and the mother jumped on Donnie and hit him repeatedly. Some of the crowd piled in. Donnie was punched and kicked and scratched and spat on. He managed to break free and run. Donnie reckoned he'd saved about 8 or 9 million people today. As he ran, Donnie thought to himself, 'I'm not sure it was worth it'.

Donnie Driftwood. Superhero. Saviour of the world. Baby murderer. Wanted criminal. Absent father.

Let's hope we don't need him again.

True story.

The Superhero ii

26

Carol could fly. Sky Girl they called her. It was her only super power. It could be used to catch people falling off buildings or bridges, I suppose. Or rescue people from burning buildings.

One day Carol walked down the road and heard some commotion. A crowd had gathered around one of the tall buildings and were looking up and pointing. At the top of the building stood a man on the ledge. Most of the crowd pulled out their smartphones, held them to the sky, and began filming. It never occurred to a single one of them to call the emergency services. *Bloody YouTube generation,* thought Carol.

The man jumped off the building and the crowd gasped. They didn't stop recording though. He hurtled towards the concrete path below, and Carol had only seconds to act.

The man hit the floor like a water balloon filled with ketchup (instead of water obviously). It was messy. Bits of brain, skull and guts everywhere. You see, Carol could fly, but she was scared of heights. Bloody useless.

What makes a hipster?

27

Joel fancied a change. He was hungry and decided to head into town for some food. As he fancied a change — the usual cafe was out of the question. So he googled *places to eat*. The smartphone asked for Joel's permission to access his location — which he thought was very polite, considerate, and ethically responsible. Well done phone. So he allowed it. The phone told him there were about 20 restaurants near his location that served food. Luckily for Joel, they were all ranked and reviewed. He decided to look at the star rating first, and narrow it down to 4 or 5 star ratings. Then, he would look at the photos customers had taken of their meals and narrowed it down to the places that looked the most visually appetising. He'd narrowed it down to 2 eateries. One was called 'The vinyl' for some reason Joel couldn't fathom, since it didn't seem to have a musical theme in the photos or description. And the other, was a restaurant called 'The Tea Tree'. Again, Joel didn't understand the naming of the restaurant. Unless they served tea tree oil as a beverage — which sounded gross and dangerous. Maybe they served tea and were particularly proud of their tea, and maybe a tree is involved in some way. Maybe they just thought it sounded good. Either way, the tea tree which had many positive reviews (more than the Vinyl) had a few really bad ones too (more than *The Vinyl)*. Apparently the staff were rude and obnoxious (according to *Karen325)*, and someone even complained that the name was stupid. So Joel made his way, using Google Maps, to *The Vinyl.*

When Joel arrived, he looked up at the wooden sign for 'The Vinyl'. It wasn't that big. It was a cross section of a tree stump, varnished, with a vinyl record attached to the centre of the stump. It didn't even have the word Vinyl printed anywhere - but it must be the place. It was next door to a coffee shop called *The Troubled Monkey*, which hadn't come up in Joel's search results. Joel thought that it looked much nicer and welcoming in *The Troubled Monkey*, but he had already decided on *The Vinyl*, and wanted to stick to his guns.

Joel walked in to *The Vinyl*, and for some reason, felt a little anxious about it. He'd already gotten the impression it would be slightly pretentious owing to the sign. He didn't like that sort of place - he felt they were very judgmental places and he felt out of place. He hadn't brought a MacBook Air or an iPad with him, so he wouldn't fit in with all the aspiring novelists and screenplay writers who chose to produce their works of genius in a coffee shop.

Joel stepped into the restaurant, or cafe/coffee shop. It definitely couldn't be described as a restaurant - it was almost certainly a cafe; a cafe with tables and chairs made out of tree stumps. *This should be called the Tea Tree,* thought Joel. There wasn't any music playing. The only vinyl you could find was stuck to the sign outside. Just as he feared, the place was littered with MacBook users with headphones in. Joel took a seat at a stump. A trendy and attractive bloke with a man-bun and glasses approached and asked him if he'd be eating today, 'Hi, my name is Carl. Can I get you a drink whilst you decide on food?' Joel said yes. The trendy hipster bloke didn't smile. He placed a menu in front of Joel before lighting a candle poking out of a wine bottle. Joel ordered a Mocha. The expressionless man walked off and Joel couldn't help but suspect those glasses were fake and the man only wore them as a fashion accessory. *Now who's being judgmental,* Joel thought to himself.

The menu was shite. Mostly vegan stuff he hadn't encountered before. He was thirty-seven years old and he couldn't believe he'd got this far in life that he didn't know what the names of all of these foods were. He recognised some of the foods though, such as 'aubergine' as he'd used the aubergine emoji loads in text messages, immature as his sense of humour was. He also recognised the foods: hummus, guacamole, and bread. That was about it. The waiter came back with a mocha and asked if Joel was ready to order food. He asked the waiter if he had scrambled egg on toast, hoping it wasn't completely vegan there and that eggs weren't considered murder. The waiter said they had eggs Benedict on sourdough. He hadn't seen this on the menu, maybe it was a secret so as not to upset the vegans. Joel said that would be great. The waiter walked away.

A waitress appeared this time, wearing a flat-cap and covered in cool tattoos. Joel appreciated tattoos but never had the confidence to get one, and now he felt he'd missed his chance and his body wasn't aesthetically pleasing enough to cover in art — he'd just be sprinkling glitter on a turd, he thought. The waitress placed a knife and fork in front of him, followed by a big jug of water with sliced cucumber in it for some reason. She placed a very, very small tumbler in front of him. He would have to refill that tumbler about ninety-seven times to get through that jug.

As Joel waited for his food, he checked his phone for messages; none. He was glad, as he wasn't feeling very sociable today. So he then checked social media. He tagged himself at *The Vinyl* using Facebook, Instagram, Twitter, and Swarm. Nobody clicked 'Like' on the check-in, which annoyed Joel. Nobody cared what he was up to.

Joel's food arrived. It was served on top of a vinyl record. 'Oh!' said Joe out loud. It all made sense now. Well, the decision to go with vinyl plates didn't make sense, but the name now did. And he hadn't heard any music since arriving. Odd for a place called *The vinyl*. It was as pretentious as he'd feared, but the food looked delicious. So Joel took a photograph of his food. He took 13 photos actually, as he wasn't happy with the first 12. He added a filter to make it look better - then posted to all of his social media accounts, subconsciously craving approval in the form of 'Likes'.

Joel ate his food and when he finished, he asked for the bill. The waiter, Carl, came back with the bill written on a clipboard-sized chalkboard. Joel was very confused. Joel got out his credit card, but the waiter immediately interrupted Joel, stating very firmly, that they only accepted bitcoin. 'What the fuck is bitcoin?' asked Joel, annoyed. The waiter explained bitcoin, leaving Joel all the more confused. After quite some argument, Joel was close to breaking point. This was ridiculous! What kind of a business doesn't accept actual money? By now, the whole waiting staff were surrounding Joel, and a manager had stepped in. The disagreement continued. The manager explained to Joel that if he couldn't pay, he would have to work off his bill. 'That's not going to happen,' snapped Joel. The manager looked to his left at the waiter and said calmly, 'Carl, would you please escort this gentleman to the hipsterfication room'.

Two hours later, a man walked into *The Vinyl,* looking up and down, and left to right, as if discovering something new and wondrous. A man with stubble, covered in tattoos, wearing dungarees, and sporting a man bun approached him and escorted him to his tree stump. He placed a menu in front of the customer. He didn't smile.

'Hi, my name is Joel. Can I get you a drink whilst you decide on food?'

The customer wondered why the waiter didn't smile.

When in Rome

28

I went to Italy for a long weekend. I'd never been and I'd always wanted to visit. I love Italian food, art, and culture. Their history is rich and you could study it your whole life and still have more to learn.

I asked a friend who had already been what I should do in Rome? She replied of course, 'When in Rome, do as the Romans do'. I laughed and left it at that.

I arrived on the Saturday, rounded up a few thousand Christians, and murdered them with fire, gladiatorial battle, and lions. It took some doing, but I got it done.

I was arrested and sent to prison for life. The judge told me I shouldn't have done what the Romans did.

Yet again *it's one rule for one, and one rule for another.*

Assassin

29

Cal Rogers was rich. He hadn't done something innovative or entrepreneurial to earn his vast wealth, unless you consider being lucky enough to be born into obscene wealth *something*. Which I doubt you do.

Cal was often bored. He hadn't done a days work in his life — so he spent most of his time indulging in his fantasies, whether they be sexual fantasies, supernatural, science fiction, or hero fantasies. What are hero fantasies? Let me explain. Cal was really into superhero films. Not just superhero films, but any hero films. Any film that involved a protagonist going up against an antagonist appealed to Cal, whether that be westerns, martial arts, spy fiction, action, or as I said before, superhero films. One of his favourite superheroes was *The Punisher*. He loved the anti-hero thing, and the idea of exacting instant justice. This was his fantasy, becoming a vigilante, and just like Batman or Ironman, he had the wealth to indulge it.

Something Cal was known for, was his self-righteousness and moral superiority complex. Despite his hero worship, Cal often wished he was in power, as, in his opinion, he would definitely sort out all of the problems in this country — especially when it came to crime. He'd make all the decisions and it wouldn't be open to debate — because he knew what was good for people. There obviously is some irony in all of this - a man who believes in heroism but also dictatorships. But that's just how it is.

So what would you do if you wanted to change society for the better and be a hero to the people? That's right - buy a sniper riffle.

Cal had been watching on the news a few months back, some football hooligans fighting in the streets, and innocent bystanders got caught up in the middle of it all. Many people were injured and the scenes were dreadful. Later that same week, there was a mass shooting in a shopping centre. Many were killed, along with the shooters when an armed-response unit arrived on the scene. A few weeks later, Cal watched on the news something that disgusted him. It was the final straw. A politician was being interviewed near Westminster Bridge, something he wasn't particularly interested in. No, it wasn't the politician that drew his attention, it was someone passing by in the background - just some bloke walking by. He walked by and just spat on the floor. Spat on the floor! Like it's a perfectly acceptable thing to do? You wouldn't walk past a tv crew and take a piss. You wouldn't squat outside Waitrose and do a shit. Why was spitting acceptable? This was it - this was the final straw. This was when Cal decided to get his sniper riffle.

It seems a slight overreaction to spitting, buying a gun. But he felt strongly about it - these people were scum and the world was better off without them. So he found out how to access the 'dark web' through some dodgy people he'd met at a swanky event last year. He thought at the time that these people were definitely mafia or whatever the British equivalent is. They were definitely criminals, he thought. When he asked what they did — they'd reply with 'oh this and that, Imports and exports. Taking care of..problems'. We all know what that means. So Cal contacted one of these dubious gentlemen and asked how he might procure a sniper rifle. As it turns out, they were *literally* involved in imports and exports; they were import and export administrators for a freight company and weren't being evasively ambiguous or trying to insinuate they were part of some insidious criminal organisation. They were literally in the import and export industry. But luckily, the guy he'd managed to reach on the phone, was still a bit dodgy. His name was Dave, and despite being somewhat shocked by Cal's imprudent request for a sniper rifle, he still replied, 'you can get anything off the dark web, mate'. And that was that. Cal had his answer. He did his research and found out how to do this dark web thing. Apparently it was quite a grim, nasty, immoral, dark, and sinful place, full of all sorts of perversions — hence the name 'dark web'. Cal thought to himself, once he's got his gun, maybe he could take out this dark web and those who use it for evil. Maybe he'd kill Dave - he seemed to know about it — so he's probably up to no good. But he didn't want to get ahead of himself. He just wanted his sniper rifle. Thanks Dave.

So his sniper rifle arrived and he opened the box like it was Christmas morning. He wondered if the Parcel Force man knew he was delivering a very expensive and illegal weapon? Nah. Anyway, it was awesome. It was a C15, otherwise known as the McMillan Tac-50. Cal had read that a Canadian sniper had set the world record for a long-distance kill, taking out his target from an astonishing 3,540 meters away; that's 2.14 miles! The Canadian had used the C15 to set this record. Cal knew this was his weapon. It came with a hefty £30,000 price tag, but Cal had spent more on a wrist watch the previous week, so he didn't care.

Cal knew that if he was going to deliver swift justice to the evil spitting scumbags in society, he'd need a plan, and a target. He heard a Neo-Nazi, far-right, white supremacist group were going on a march next weekend. This was perfect. They would undoubtedly go on a rampage and attack innocent bystanders. Plus, they were vile, hateful scum, whether they were violent or not. The world would be a better place without them. So Cal had until the weekend to get a plan together.

He had it! It came to him as he was falling asleep one night. What he needed next was a drone. A drone that could carry plenty of weight, and could move at great speed. Nothing on eBay or Amazon would do the trick. He'd need to find a drone up to the task, and order quickly, in time to carry out his plan - his justice. Cal stayed up all night researching drones. He finally found one - it was a beast! A pricey beast at that - costing him a whopping $20,749.90. He'd had to order it from the US, and he didn't care what it cost in pounds sterling, so he didn't do the conversion. He was rich remember. He'd need to adapt the drone slightly, but nothing requiring an engineering degree, just the fixation of two hooks to carry a bag.

Next, he needed a fake tattoo sleeve, the kind that slips on and off like a pair of tights, but on your arm. He also ordered two new rucksacks, a sports cap, two hoodies, some tracksuit bottoms and a new pair of jeans. Two new pairs of trainers ,and some sunglasses were also in order. Apart from the tattoo stuff, he already owned all these things, but he was getting carried away. He even ordered a cool-looking face-mask that made him look like a character from Naruto or some other manga show; he didn't want to sneeze during his mission and leave his DNA everywhere. Nor did he want to leave fingerprints, so he bought some leather gloves, which he'd seen assassins wearing in the films he'd watched. He finished off his spending spree by buying some bath salts, which he found relaxing and he'd run out of last week.

Cal spent the rest of the week researching the area in which the thugs were supposed to be 'protesting'. He physically walked around, checked out buildings, entrances and exits, alleys, CCTV cameras, and anything that might help or hinder his mission. He used Google Earth to check out rooftops and roads. He found out where the roadblocks would be and speculated where police would likely be placed.

The big day arrived. Cal hadn't slept at all — it was like Christmas and he was an excited 10 year old. He'd seen the news and the Neo-Nazis were gathered at their starting point and were due to begin their march. Cal had to get to their end point — where he suspected the majority of the violence would take place. He put on a t-shirt, followed by his fake tattoo sleeve, which fit nicely along the entire length of his arm. He placed a smaller rucksack into his larger rucksack, along with his cap, face-mask, two hoodies, and his tracksuit bottoms. He crammed his gloves into his jeans' pockets. Cal was ready to go.

When he got close to the building he'd settled on, he popped on his face-mask. There were face-masks everywhere owing to a global pandemic. You may remember it. He stepped into the public building, which was currently allowing visitors, as long as they didn't go near each other. Cal had found it hard to find a good spot for his mission, but this place had a restaurant on the top floor - which gave him the perfect excuse for getting in. When he got to the top floor, he now had to get to the roof. This was tricky, as the door to the roof was chained shut and secured with the Hulk of all padlocks. Cal hadn't thought of this and panicked. His meticulous plan was already out the window. Damn it! In his frantic desperation, Cal began shaking and yanking the bar handle on the door, the kind you get on fire escape doors. The door opened! The chain and padlock obviously remained in tact, but whoever had secured the chain, hadn't done a good job of it because the door was ajar just enough for a slim person to squeeze through - so Cal did just that. What a stroke of luck.

On the roof, Cal walked over to the ledge. Already waiting for him, a long sports bag was resting on the floor, attached to two hooks attached to his drone, which was parked next to the bag. It had made a perfect landing.

Cal zipped open the bag and removed his riffle. He opened his rucksack and took out the smaller bag, which contained a pair of trainers and a pair of sunglasses. He removed the other bits and bobs, took off his jeans, and slipped into the tracksuit bottoms and one of the hoodies. The fake tattoo sleeve slid off and was tossed into the small rucksack. He placed on his cap, assassin gloves — which were actually driving gloves, and removed his face-mask. He was ready.

The sniper riffle was placed onto a tripod for stability. Cal had practised for days in his garden and seemed to be a natural — there was no way he could miss. He lay down on his belly prone, shuffled forward positioning himself closer to the riffle, and placed his right eye against the sight. He could see the thugs in the distance, and as expected, they were kicking off. Police were holding the line, but the Nazis were slamming into them, some throwing punches, and some throwing projectiles. Cal didn't want to waste any time — he could probably take out a fair few of them before having to make his escape. By the time anyone had figured out where the shots had come from, he'd be long gone.Cal could see almost a mile away using his riffle's telescopic sight. The crosshairs hovered over the head of one of the skinheads at the back of the mob. His reasoning was that if he took them out from the back, the front wouldn't know what was happening, giving him enough time to take them out one by one, working his way to the front. If he'd started at the front, the thugs behind them would panic and flee. It'd be much harder to hit moving targets. So this was it, the big moment, the beginning of his career as a vigilante. Cal steadied his sight — the skinhead's head was wobbling back and forth as he yelled and chanted with the horde. But Cal stayed steady, every time the skinhead's head moved out of his crosshairs, it would move back again after a second. He just had to time it right. The head moved forward, then back into the crosshairs - Cal took his shot. The bullet flew through the air gracefully, and reached its target a very short moment after leaving the barrel. It pierced the man's cranium at his temple and burst out the other side, creating an explosive mess of brain, blood and bone which splattered the left side of another fella's face. It took a second for the man coated in bits of the skinhead's brain to realise what had happened - probably the time it took for the skinhead's body to hit the ground. As Cal was so far away, the sound of the gun firing wasn't as audible to the mob as you might think. So the thugs at the front of the crowd hadn't really noticed. Cal aimed and took another shot. He missed the thug he was aiming for but still hit someone else who dropped like a sack of shit as they say. He took another shot, and another, and another, working his way towards the front as he'd planned. By the time he got to the front, the majority of the crowd had dispersed and were running for their lives. The front rows had noticed something was wrong, but Cal had managed to take out a couple of them before they legged it. He'd singled out the one's at the front who were throwing punches - he particular hated them. Cal had managed to take out nine hooligans. It wasn't many - but it was more than enough.

 Cal packed away his riffle, and placed it into his sports bag. He pulled out a control pad from the sports bag before zipping it up. He tapped a few buttons and the drone took off, lifting the sports bag carrying the riffle into the air. He tapped a few more buttons and the drone flew off. The drone had a GPS 'return to base' function; all Cal had to do was activate it, and it would return home. He took off his gloves and shoved them into the small rucksack, along with the face-mask and clothes. He folded the larger rucksack tightly and crammed it into the smaller one with difficulty.

He made his way out of the building. He could hear multiple sirens in the distance. Cal had his escape route planned. He walked down the road, and turned into an alley behind some shops. There were plenty of bins for Cal to ditch a few things. He changed into his second hoody, tossing the one he'd been wearing into the bin. He threw the larger of the rucksacks into the bin too, along with the gloves, tattoo sleeve, cap, and jeans. He removed his trainers and replaced them with another pair. He slipped on his sunglasses and walked calmly from the alley onto the road and made his way home, stopping for a takeaway coffee along the way.

Cal arrived home and was greeted by a number of men in suits, and about 12 uniformed police officers. They seized him and arrested him, pinning him to the floor whilst doing so.

'How did you find me?' Cal demanded — furious his meticulous planning hadn't saved him.

'We followed that massive drone carrying that huge sports bag' replied one of the suited men.

'Agh shit', mumbled Cal.

Nihilist

30

....

John's therapist sat in his leather armchair with his legs crossed, holding a notebook and pen. He looked over his spectacles at John, who sat on a black leather sofa twiddling his thumbs and biting his nails interchangeably. The room was minimalist. The walls were maroon and the ceiling a dull white. Behind the therapist was a large bay window looking out across a bright green park. To John's left was a bookshelf full of academic literature and textbooks. To his right, the wall was all but bare; all but the therapist's framed qualification, firmly screwed into the wall.

The therapist popped his pen into his mouth, paused, then took it out again - not once averting his intense gaze away from John. The therapist jotted something down on his notepad, smiled, and removed his glasses before looking back at John. The therapist asked John if he felt any improvement in his mental state since their last session.

'Oh my God, life is tedious. It's tedious and merciless and relentless and meaningless. It's all those words; the ones ending in 'less'. Pointless, hopeless, worthless, fruitless, useless, aimless, profitless, godless, ruthless, and valueless', said John.

'So that's a no then?'

'Of course it's a fucking no!' snapped John.

'This nihilist persona you've created isn't fooling anyone John. A true nihilist has no belief in purpose or meaning. Existential nihilism would have us believe that life has no value or meaning; that you are insignificant, and nothing, absolutely nothing matters in all existence. You are pessimistic, granted. But a nihilist you are not. So, I am calling your bluff John. If you truly believed nothing mattered and that you are truly insignificant and of no value whatsoever, then you'd probably kill yourself. And that dear John, we simply can not — '

BANG!

John had revealed a handgun he'd been hiding under his t-shirt, partially tucked into his trousers, put it to his head and pulled the trigger. His brain, bits of skull and a gallon of blood was now splattered over and seeping into a plethora of academic textbooks on psychology, psychiatry, mental health, and philosophy. The therapist hadn't read any of them.

'He forgot needless. And senseless', added the therapist, jotting down his thoughts and massaging his chin with his spare hand. 'I wonder how many other words ending in "less" I can think of?'

He thought of two more.

He buzzed his secretary, 'Gill, better cancel my twelve o'clock and call the cleaners. It happened again'.

The itch

31

Fran had an itch. It had been bothering her all day, and she'd scratched it so much that her arm was now red raw. When Fran got home from work, she rolled up her cardigan sleeve and looked at the inflamed arm. She cringed at how much damage she'd done to her own arm through scratching alone. But it was still itchy, and she couldn't control her urge to scratch it.

As she scratched the itch, her mind went into speculation mode. *Was I bitten? No, I've been bitten before, it doesn't feel like a bite. Is it just an itch, an everyday itch? No, I know what that feels like and this wasn't that. So maybe the horribly prickly-heat itch you get from getting sun burnt?* No, as tortuous as that is, Fran knew what it felt like, and this was not that.

So she scratched again. And again. And again and again, until we were no longer in skin territory, we were in adipose tissue territory. She could see the fatty tissue, all yellowy and soft. It looked disgusting, and blood kept seeping out over the fat and back into it, like a sponge absorbing water. Fran continued to scratch her itch, which wasn't going anywhere despite the skin having been scratched away. How could she still be feeling an itch without any skin? Does fatty tissue get itchy? The fatty tissue had been annihilated and now she was scratching what was left — muscle, tendons, and blood vessels. It was a bloody mess. Fran thought maybe she'd finally reach a huge nerve, and that would be the end of the itch, but no. The itch remained. Fran peeled off the rest of the skin on her forearm and hand, like she was removing a glove. It was just getting in the way of her itching.

After the de-gloving, Fran was panicked and scared — but it was too late, she'd scratched away her own flesh, and defeating the itch was all that mattered now; now that there was only bone left.

Fran frantically scratched away at both long bones in her forearm and something caught her eye. On her bone was etched the words, 'and you're awake — the itch is gone and you're back in the room'. And the itch was gone! Just like that! Completely gone! Finally! But that was not all; Fran noticed something very odd indeed. Something odd between her bones. She was no expert, but she was pretty sure it wasn't supposed to be there. It was a folded up piece of card, wedged between the radius and ulna. Fran reached in, removed the card, and unfolded it carefully. It was a playing card. It was the ace of hearts!

As Fran bled out from her open wound, she remembered the magician she'd been to see the night before. He specialised in magic and hypnosis. Fran had been dragged up onto the stage and shown a card trick. It didn't work. When the magician held up a card and said, 'is this your card?' Fran replied with an unimpressed 'no'. The magician apologised and sent her back to her seat. He'd failed to hypnotise her too, so she left doubly disappointed. His tricks seemed to work on others, as did his hypnosis, but nothing worked on her. Fran thought that she was maybe too strong-willed for any of that nonsense. So now, in the present moment, Fran stared at the Ace of Hearts, which had etched on it in permanent marker, 'Is this your card?'.

'Yes! Yes it is! That's the card! That's my bloody card! That's amazing! Bloody hell he's good!' exclaimed Fran, before collapsing onto the floor into a puddle of her own blood.

Infinite Monkeys

32

The infinite monkey theorem is a fascinating one. It states that a monkey, given an infinite length of time (and providing the monkey is immortal) could produce the entire works of Shakespeare. I suppose trillions upon trillions of years down the line, the poor exhausted monkey could just so happen to randomly type the keys in just the right order to fluke the entire works of Shakespeare, although it'd be just as impressive for said monkey to produce just one of his sonnets.

So the theorem, I suppose, says something mind boggling about probability (or improbability), as well as eternity. I looked it up and one figure given for the chance of the monkey producing Hamlet alone, was $4.4 \times 10^{360,783}$.

So that's damn near impossible. Four point four multiplied by ten, three hundred and sixty-thousand, seven hundred and eighty-three times. Maybe I'm explaining it badly, or misinterpreting the information — but all you need to know really, is it's nigh on impossible.

But what happened was, the editor of some physics journal decided one day to produce a light-hearted front cover that clearly referenced the infinite monkey theorem, so he organised for a chimpanzee to sit at a table with a typewriter on it. He placed glasses on the monkey to suggest intelligence, which didn't make sense because the monkey was supposed to represent randomness without intelligence. But it looked funny.

So the monkey sat there, sporting his spectacles, with his fingers on the typewriter, looking at the camera, and not really paying much attention to what he was supposed to be doing. The photoshoot took ages because the monkey just wouldn't behave. He ate quite a lot of paper and picked up the typewriter and threw it at Dave the cameraman quite a few times. After a while they replaced Dave the cameraman; as it turned out the monkey wasn't a fan. He preferred Dave's replacement Simon. He didn't throw the typewriter at Simon. So eventually, the monkey bashed his hands over the typewriter in just the right way to get a photo that made it appear that he was typing. But once the photoshoot was over, the monkey picked his nose, ate his bogey, and kept tapping away at the keyboard. The team decided to leave the monkey to it whilst they all went on a break.

When they eventually came back, the monkey's handler stepped into the enclosed room where the monkey sat, still typing. She approached him and reached out to remove the typewriter, but the monkey snarled at her and continued to type. The handler decided to leave him be, leaving some food on the table, before leaving and settling on returning the next day.

The next day, the team, including the handler, returned to the room to find the monkey leaning back in his chair snoring away. They all smiled. Then, upon closer inspection, the handler and the editor looked down at the typed up paper, then back at each other in disbelief. He'd only gone and bloody done it! He'd written the entire works of William Shakespeare. He'd also defecated on the keys.

The monkey wasn't a special monkey or anything, he just fluked it. Maybe the odds of a monkey typing out the entire works of Shakespeare in a trillion trillion years time, are the same as typing it out next Wednesday, or tomorrow. But he'd done it pretty quickly.

This was a major event. The physics journal dedicated their entire publication that month to this miraculous event. This would change the world, they said.

But nobody believed them.

True story. Well, inspired by true events.

Want to live forever?

33

In the future, mankind will overcome the disease that is mortality. There will come a time when our genetics can be modified in one way or another, resulting in eternal life. Maybe we'll pop a pill. Maybe some complicated procedure will take place. We'll live for hundreds and hundreds of years, perhaps thousands, before meeting some gruesome end, because a traumatic event or tragic accident will be the only thing that kills us.

But my what big ears and big noses we'll have!

As we age, these are the only body parts that don't stop growing.

Our future world will be overrun with big noses. And big ears. People with massive ears and massive noses will be everywhere. It's going to be really weird and I'm not sure people will be attracted to each other anymore, so sexual intercourse will no longer exist. Not because people are superficial in the future, but because their noses will be so big that you can't really see their faces at all. And their ears will look like they're sticking out of the sides of their giant noses. So people will look like walking noses — and those noses will have ears.

Think on.

Diarrhoea

34

Joey had diarrhoea.

He sat on the toilet for an hour — a relentlessly draining hour. It just wouldn't stop.

But then it did. And Joey had a shower because he felt pretty disgusting and unclean — all the wiping in the world couldn't cleanse his butt-hole.

After the shower, Joey popped into the living room to relax watching the tv. He vowed never to drink so much ever again — thinking the copious volumes of lager he'd poured down his gullet might offer some explanation as to why his insides seemed to be exploding out of his arsehole. Oh and there was the kebab — there was something off about that kebab, albeit delicious.

A knock came at the door. He answered promptly, but as he stood up, a loud grumbling in his belly made itself known, and he knew he'd need to get to the toilet again, and fast. He'd just need to get rid of whoever was at the door first. He answered, and Todd stood there looking annoyed. 'Mate - what's going on? We were supposed to meet over an hour ago. And you haven't been answering my texts. Seriously man — what the fuck?'
Todd never got angry — and he wasn't now — but it was as close to it as Joey had ever seen him get.
'What are you talking about?' Joey asked, looking behind him intermittently - still longing for the toilet at the end of the hallway.

'We were supposed to be going to the match. I've been waiting in the Nell for ages! Can I come in or what?

'Now's not a good time. Sorry mate, I'm hungover as fuck. I haven't even checked my phone, and I can't stop shitting. Sorry dude, I promise I'll make it up to you next time!'

'Yeah you'd better. Let me in then, we can still catch the second half on the telly'. Todd made a move for the doorway, but Joey stepped forward and wedged himself into the gap blocking Todd's path.

'What are you doing?' Todd's pitch went high and he frowned, ageing him 10 years as his Gordon Ramsey crumpled up forehead appeared.

'I've got the shits! I need to go! I need to go right now or else I'm gonna - ' Joey paused, his eyes widened and a look of horror overwhelmed his pale face. 'Oh shit!' He said.

'You've followed through haven't you?' Todd wasn't annoyed anymore - he had a massive grin on his face.

'm-m-maybe' came the broken reply.

'I'll let you go then. Jesus man - you need to reign in the drinking. And is it me or do you look shorter?'

'What are you on about? Fuck off will you - I'll call you later' There was desperation in Joey's voice, who slammed the door in his best friend's face.

Joey pegged it to the toilet, he could feel the follow-through trickling down the inside of his leg like one of those fancy coffee machines dispensing an espresso shot. He slipped his trousers and pants down to his ankles, and slammed his arse cheeks onto the toilet seat, and proceeded to blast the bowl with high-pressured fluidic shite. 'Oh God it was draining' thought Joey. He felt his energy being sapped and his head slumped forward in exhaustion.

'And what the fuck did Todd mean I looked shorter?' Joey thought to himself.

Joey took about 45 minutes that time. He rummaged through the medicine cabinet looking for diarrhoea tablets and finally found some at the back. He glanced at the instructions on the back, before promptly popping two pills with a glass of water. Joey slid the medicine cabinet shut, revealing his reflection in the sliding mirror. Joey tip-toed to see his whole face, and he looked rough. He looked tired and drained. *Hold on a minute! What the fuck?* Joey felt a wave of panic move through him. His belly filled with butterflies and he felt a kind of swelling of fear in his head — like a headache but with dizziness and blurred vision. It was the kind of panic you'd feel upon discovering a lump where no lump should be — like in your balls or something. You see, Joey had never had to tip-toe to see himself in the mirror before. *Had someone moved the cabinet higher up the wall as a practical joke?* He lived alone, but Todd did come over a lot and it was just the sort of prank he might play. And Todd did say he looked shorter, setting up the joke perfectly. No, Todd only appeared because Joey hadn't shown up for the match. And when did Todd ever spend long enough in the toilet to take a cabinet down, move it higher, and screw it in again — requiring some drilling that Joey would definitely have heard. Joey scrambled for his bits n' bobs drawer in the hallway and retrieved a permanent marker. He stood with his back against the wall, and paying no regard to his nice newly painted wall, scribbled a line above his head marking his current height. Then, the grumbling in his belly returned. He was going to find a tape measure to measure the distance from floor to the line on the wall, but there wasn't enough time. His guts rumbling like a bariatric belly before a McDonalds binge. He shot to the loo again - parked his arse down on the seat, and destroyed the poor bowl. The exhaustion was horrible. Tears slid down his cheeks. Then came a loud plop. It sounded too loud for runny shit, and he hadn't passed a solid all morning. He flexed his head forward and down, peering between his thighs into the bowl. Oh my God! A large red bloody mass filled the bowl. It looked like the Liver he'd had for dinner the night before last. But it couldn't be *his* liver - or else he'd be dead. Was it something else? Had he got to the point where he couldn't shit out runny shite anymore, and all that was left were internal organs? But which organ? Surely he needed his organs? Maybe the reason he wasn't dead was because it was his appendix or something. No, his appendix would be smaller. *Spleen? No, you can't shit out your own organs. Can you?* Whatever it was, it wasn't good. Finally, the experience came to a close. He couldn't pass anything more and he was drained. He flushed and the water drained, leaving the mystery organ just sitting there. Joey was worried. He was very worried.

 Joey rushed to the landline on the telephone table in the hallway. Yes, he still had a landline. But there were odder things happening right now for us to delve into that oddness. As he reached for the phone, he glanced over to the line he'd scribbled on the wall. Shit! No way? It looked higher than before. Well, higher than him. He had to look up — quite a bit. He turned from the phone, snatched up the marker pen, and rushed to the wall, turning his back to it and scribbling yet another line above his head. He promptly turned to face the wall, and to his horror, the second line was below the previous, by a good foot!

 Joey was scared — more scared than he'd ever been before. He headed back to the telephone but suddenly his insides rumbled. Shit! It was a third wave. He rushed to the toilet and emptied a few pints of liquid brown. It was back to being runny. He knew he had to get help. He fumbled for his mobile phone but he'd left it upstairs — he needed to call an ambulance but it would have to wait, he had to stay on the toilet until the next respite. A shite respite; a shitespite, if you will.

It didn't stop. Joey was sweating heavily from his brow and he felt weaker than he'd ever felt before. He could barely support himself on the toilet. He even felt like he was falling into it. Finally, it stopped. Joey took a sigh of relief, wiped his arse as best he could, not worrying too much about the quality of his work considering he'd probably be back again in a minute or two, and hopped down off the toilet. He reached up to the sink to wash his hands, dried them off on the hand towel, and reached up to the door handle to leave the toilet. *Hold on! What's all this reaching up?* Joey panicked. He ran back to the hallway, grabbed his marker pen, and drew another line above his head. He was shocked. The line was much lower than the previous lines. It was a good 2 foot lower than the last!

Then came the rumbling again. He rushed to the loo. He had to run and jump to reach the toilet door handle, and climbed, using all of his remaining strength, onto the toilet seat. Then came the trots again. It was horrible, painful, exhausting, and terrifying. He looked back down between his little legs that were braced between the sides of the seat to stop him falling in, and saw what looked like offal. He could have sworn he'd seen his kidneys in there. He panicked, jumped off the seat, whilst blood and espresso poo dribbled down his thigh, and ran to the hallway. He looked up at the lines. He wanted to draw another but he'd left the marker pen on the telephone table and he couldn't reach it anymore. He also wanted to use the phone to get help, but he couldn't reach that either. Suddenly, he felt a short sharp cramp in his belly. He ran to the toilet once more, and jumped as high as he could to get onto the seat, failing the first two attempts. He finally managed to climb up and perch himself so his bum was dangling over the bowl, whilst he held onto the front of the seat with his little hands. He was no bigger than a kitten now. Imagine a kitten trying to do a poo on a toilet without falling in; it's kind of like that, but instead of a shitting kitten, it's a tiny shitting man.

Joey cried. He cried and cried and cried some more. He cried out for help, but no one would come - his cries were no louder than a mouse's squeak.

The shitting didn't stop, and Joey felt himself shrinking away. He pulled himself up and thrust himself forward so he landed on the tiled floor; there was no way he was going to die in his own shit in his own toilet bowl. As he lay there on the floor, the size of a finger puppet, he continued to shit — it was gross. He reached out, placed his hand in his own excrement, accepting the undignified death he'd tried to avoid, and scribed something out on the floor, before finally, disappearing completely between atoms.

Todd came over the next day as he hadn't heard back from Joey and he wasn't answering his phone. Worried he was ill, Todd forced his way in. The place stunk! As he walked throughout the house, calling out Joey's name, he paused at the toilet door. The smell was stronger here. He cautiously pushed the door open and saw the state of the toilet bowl. He looked down and saw excrement on the tiled floor. It looked like somebody had smeared it into a word. In the shittiest font ever, the word 'kebab' had been spelt out in tiny brown letters. Todd shook his head and said out loud, 'The dirty bastard'.

The Island of Peace and Love

35

There was an experiment. It was designed by a group of disillusioned scientists in the hope of creating a better society. It was also pretty damn unethical.

On the 1st of January 1947 our scientists had already put into motion the most ambitious social experiment in modern history. Following the atrocities of the second world war, the world was shocked at the cruelty mankind was capable of, and some of the finest minds of the 20th century decided to act.

On the same day, 25 babies from across the globe were taken from their parents at birth, and raised together by the scientists until they could walk, speak, and show basic social skills such as kindness, sharing, playing, and talking. The scientists, along with their partners, all lived in the same commune and as part of the experiment, weren't allowed to show any signs of conflict, aggression, favouritism, discrimination or emotional extremes. The group of children were never separated, and there was never any mention of brothers, sisters, mothers, or fathers. No one child was raised by one particular adult. It was found early on that some of the children favoured certain scientists, but this was discouraged on the whole.

The children were selected specifically to represent as diverse a sample of the world's population. They wanted a variety of demographics from every continent. Diversity was the key theme.

Divisions between race and culture was apparent throughout society and the experiment aimed to prove that prejudice, hate, racism, and bigotry in general, was learned behaviour and a systemic failure. Humanity was failing its children with a perpetual cycle of prejudice passed down from generation to generation. The scientists knew this, and there was plenty of research backing it up. Unfortunately, there was no experiment that proved mankind could co-exist without any of these problems.

The funding for this experiment came from multiple governments — the budget was huge; so huge that an entire island was leased in the mediterranean for it to take place on. When the children reached the age of 6, they were transported to the island, which had, over the course of the preceding 6 years, been transformed into a habitat capable of enabling self-sufficiency. Only two scientists would be allowed to accompany the children to their new home, to teach the children to be self-sufficient and thrive, before leaving them permanently to fend for themselves.

The children's childhoods were cut short — the scientists needed to raise them at a greater rate than your average child in order to prepare them for their abandonment. As prepubescents go, they were well-educated and sensible, loving and compassionate. Their education, albeit a shamefully censored one, was perfectly designed to enable self-sufficiency and cooperation without prejudice.

They were educated well and prepared for anything. They were taught on the subjects of science, literature, mathematics, technology, music, and art. The subject of history was carefully considered; and it was decided that certain historical events and figures should be omitted from their education, in fear that this could draw attention to differences between the children, resulting in division or isolation. The scientists didn't want one particular group resenting another for how their ancestors were treated, or how their biological families in their respective communities continue to be failed by society and marginalised to this day. This had to be hidden for the sake of the experiment. An ethics board would never approve.

The children were left on the island to fend for themselves when they all reached 12 years of age.

The children lived in a community, worked, played, lived off the bountiful land, and grew up into adults. They paired off, fell in love, and in time had children of their very own; all whilst maintaining a close community,

The scientists studied the new and growing society, remaining hidden at all times. The island had more CCTV per square-metre than anywhere else in the world. Spy-planes were used to fly overhead to survey the community and map its growth and development. No signs of conflict were spotted. Eventually, the rest of the world lost interest in the experiment, the scientists in charge disappeared into obscurity, CCTV left in disrepair, and the islanders left to their own devices. There was no profit to be made — and investment in the experiment dried up.

It was now the year 2016 and a renewed interest in the historical social experiment emerged, gaining extreme momentum on social media. Investment flooded in again. CCTV was repaired and swarms of drones were used to spy on the islanders.

It was then decided that the outside world should make contact with the inhabitants. They would be the ancestors of the original 25 children, and maybe even some of the original 25 were still alive. One man was selected as an ambassador. He had a proven track record in making first contact with remote and isolated tribes — taking risks that most were unwilling to take. He was a scientist, philosopher, psychologist, archeologist, and historian. He'd lost track of how many qualifications he had, and considered himself somewhat of an Indiana Jones figure, although his name was pretty plain and disappointing; John Smith.

John Smith arrived on the island bearing many gifts such as, chocolate, cake, fruit, toys, clothes, gadgets, books, music, and new medicines, although the community was generally a healthy one.

John Smith greeted the community. He discovered early on that a system of hierarchy had been established and noted that a tribal-leader had been selected in a form of democracy that impressed John. There seemed to be no conflict or divisions. Marriages had taken place, and John observed many couples that proved diversity didn't have to be a problem in a society. There was no issues surrounding ethnicity in this society - marriages and births reflected this. There was no issues of homophobia, and marriages reflected this. Men married men, and women married women. In fact, gender was barely acknowledged - being seen as a spectrum of variability rather than a limited two choice tradition. Fluidity of gender was apparent. Relationships were monogamous and polygamous. Children were raised in the community, with each parent caring for not only her own offspring, but also those of their community. John was surprised at how tribal the community had become, having studied the original experiment and noting the abandonment of the modern community they'd been bequeathed. Nonetheless, the community thrived.

John had been welcomed most affectionately and after many months amongst the inhabitants, it was time to leave. On his last day, the community had surprised John with a feast, musical performances, and story-telling. After the day's entertainment, the tribal leader informed John there was one last tradition they'd like him to enjoy. John was happy his last day was such a joyous occasion and overwhelmed by the kindness and affection he'd been gifted.

The community gathered, men, women, non-binary, children et al. They led John along a trail, and hiked up a steep hill to the peak. Trees and overgrown plants greeted them, and one by one, community members passed through a narrow opening between green overgrowth. Finally, John made his way through the narrow space and into a wide open area of land, the floor was baron, just dried-out soil out of which no plant life could grow. The trees surrounded them in a circular fashion like a Greek amphitheatre. Rows and rows of benches surrounded them in parallel with the trees, upon which many of the community were already seated. In front of John was a blinding fire, emanating from a huge, tall wooden structure. John recoiled in horror at the terrible sight. He couldn't believe his eyes. The fire — it was burning intensely — burning a body. He looked away in disgust. As he looked back, some of the men and women were pulling ropes attached to other wooden structures. They'd constructed huge wooden stakes to crucify people. As they pulled and raised the structures to a standing state, he could hear the voices of those nailed to the crosses — they were begging for their lives and screaming. Some of the community walked over to the raised structures, and holding torches they leant down to the dried kindling at the bases, and set alight the crosses. The screams were horrifying and John wretched until he vomited. The crowd cheered. Even the children cheered, and it appalled John to the core.

'What did you do?' cried John, addressing the leader.
'What do you mean?' came his curious reply.
'Why are you burning these people?'
'Oh - they're abominations'
'Abominations?!' John recoiled.
'Yeah - you know, those with vile disgusting red and orange hair'
'You mean gingers?!'
'Oh you have them too?'
'You're burning gingers! Oh my God!'
'Well, yeah. Don't you?'
'God no!
'Oh. Why not?'
'Because it's inhumane. I can't believe this! How did this happen? What led you all down this evil path?'
'What's evil?'
'It's this! It's fucking this!'
'Oh'
'You murder people in the most excruciating way because of the colour of their hair!'
'I'm very confused by your reaction, John'
'This experiment is a total failure'

'But there's more to come! We haven't begun the elder executions yet.'

'What the fuck are the elder executions?'

'Well, when our people reach 50, we execute them. They become a burden. Our community has to stay at a stable population size. It's ok - they all agree to it - it's been a tradition for generations'

'Ok I'm leaving'

John simply turned around and walked away that evening. He waited by the shore all night for his boat to arrive. He could see the smoke from the burning gingers rising up in the distance. He didn't say goodbye to the community. John's therapy cost in excess of £125,000 and he never truly recovered from his ordeal. He never wrote up his findings. Many gingers lost their lives.

Fairies

36

'Do you want me to read you a bedtime story?' asked Alice, quite adorably, as she pulled the duvet up to her chin and shuffled up a bit higher in the bed so her head was comfortably burrowed into her big pink pillow.

'Shouldn't it be the other way round?' replied Tony, sitting on the edge of the bed, tucking her in tightly.

'Well, you always read the stories. So I think it's my turn Daddy' said the logical 5 year old.

'Well, you've got me there sweetheart. What are you going to read me?'

'I'll just tell it because I remember it, I think it's better that way' came the authoritative reply from the 5 year old.

'Ok, so you're not going to read me a story, you're going to tell me a story' Dad replied sarcastically.

'No! I am going to read you a story, but from my mind' came the sharp reply from his unimpressed daughter. She didn't like his tone.

'I'm sorry honey — of course you are. I can't wait. What story are you going to read me?' said Dad, hoping to undo the damage he'd done with the sarcasm that hadn't gone unnoticed by his daughter.

'Well, Daddy. I am going to read you the story of the fairy hospital'

Tony smiled to himself. His daughter made him so proud and her imagination always managed to impress him. He leaned in and kissed her on the forehead and replied, 'What's the story of the fairy hospital?'.

'Well,' Alice began.

Alice often began sentences with the word, 'Well,' which made it sound like she was about to reveal the most juicy gossip in town, but usually it would be something pretty normal like, 'Well, I don't want cornflakes today' or 'Well, I prefer the blue one'. Although once she did reveal some juicy gossip regarding the neighbours (Mr Jones) at number 42 whom she said had been 'letting a lot of different ladies in his house whenever Mrs Jones leaves for work,' before asking if the ladies were 'coming to stop him being lonely whilst Mrs Jones was at her job?'

'Sort of' replied Tony, at the time praying there'd be no follow-up questions.

Alice, cleared her throat and continued,

'The world is full of fairies because the world is magical. The magical fairies make good things happen. They leave money under your pillow when you lose a tooth. They're called tooth fairies. And others grant wishes. Some of them just watch over you and make sure you're ok. But one day, all of the fairies had to visit the hospital. They had to visit because their fairy friend was there. All the fairies had their jobs to do, but they couldn't do them because their fairy friend was poorly. She had cancer and was having cweamafewapee'

'She must mean chemotherapy' thought Tony, whilst simultaneously feeling a little shocked and worried that his 5 year old daughter had heard of cancer and chemotherapy.

'Are you listening Daddy?' Alice asked rather irritably. Tony cleared his throat and looked at his daughter after being lost in thought for a few seconds as he digested the story.

'Yes of course love, carry on sweetie' said Tony, wondering if he should nip this story in the bud. Alice continued,

'So they visited her and took her flowers and used their magic to cheer her up. But she couldn't be cheered up. Because she had cancer. So they all went off back to their magical jobs and carried on doing fairy things. The tooth fairy then had to go back to the hospital to put money under his fairy friend's hospital pillow because the cweamafewapee had made all of her teeth fall out. So the sick fairy had lots of money but couldn't spend it. So she gave it to the nurses. But then the fairy died of cancer and the other fairies were sad. And the nurses were sad, but happy about the money. The End' announced Alice calmly with a look of pride on her face.

'Wow. That was great sweetie. Erm, where did you hear about cancer and all that stuff?' Tony asked calmly, he didn't want Alice to think she was in trouble.

'Oh it was at swimming. Oscar's Daddy has it and he died and his hair and teeth fell out and he went to hospital and he died. I don't know whether he's still dead, but he was dead last Saturday when I saw Oscar in the pool. He told me so'.

'Oh my God! I didn't know that,' Tony paused. 'Well, sweetie, I want you to get some sleep now ok. We probably should talk about Oscar's Daddy tomorrow' Tony smiled at Alice, leant in and kissed her forehead as he had done so earlier. 'Now go to sleep. Night night'.

Tony reached over and switched the bedside lamp off. The light from the hallway allowed in just enough light to alleviate Alice's fear of the dark.

'Night night, Daddy' Alice replied.

Tony ruffled Alice's hair, then got up off the bed and walked towards the bedroom door. He pulled the door half shut, before stopping and poking his head back in. He whispered, 'Sweetie?'

'What, Daddy?' Alice whispered back.

'Why didn't the poorly fairy use magic to make herself better?' asked a curious Tony, not satisfied with such a grim ending.

'Because Daddy, not all fairies are magical; some just have cancer'

Never before had Tony been so deflated and saddened by a sentence as he had that night by his own child. Usually he'd leave that room every night with a warm, proud, and happy feeling. Not tonight; tonight he just felt creeped out.

'Night, Alice,' said Tony.
'Night, Daddy,' said Alice.

Crush

37

Ever had a crush on someone so bad that you can't stop thinking about them? Course you have. Do we even call it a crush in this country? I can't remember. It's hard to tell nowadays - so many americanisms have snuck into our language that I can't remember which words are ours and which words are theirs. I suppose it doesn't matter. So what I mean is, have you ever fancied anyone so much that it hurts? Of course you have. Well, I do. Right now. And it's worse - they don't like me. You've been there too, right? Of course you have.

I feel better that you've been there too. It's crazy the things we do when we fancy someone this much. I suppose infatuation is the best word for it. So have you ever fancied someone so much that you find any excuse to talk to them at work? Maybe go out of your way, up 4 flights of stairs and down a long corridor or something? Maybe you'll phone their office and say 'sorry, wrong number! Oh, is that you Liam? How's things? Up to much this weekend?' Of course you have.

So have you ever fancied someone so much that you've found them on every single social media platform on the internet? Of course you have. And browsed every photo posted on their instagram account going back 8 years? And checked out their Facebook photos, and even checked out their relationship status. And also, anyone in any of their photos with their arm around them — you check them out — browse through their photos and make sure they're just friends and not competition. Of course you have.

And checked their tweets for an idea of what their views might be on a range of subjects. Are they intelligent? Funny? Of course they are. And of course you have.

So have you ever fancied someone so much that you find out what they like, where they drink, what they eat, where they eat, and what coffee they prefer? Of course you have. It's a skinny mocha by the way. But you know that.

Have you ever fancied someone so much that you follow them on a night out? At the weekend? On their way home after work? And met their pets in their house whilst they're out? Oh, and have you ever fancied someone so much that you break into their house? Of course you have; how else would you meet their pets?

Have you ever fancied someone so much that you watch them sleep? Or sniff their underpants? Of course you have.

Have you ever fancied someone so much, that you have to tie them up in your basement so that they never leave you? And you have to write them a letter explaining why you can't let them go, and how much you fancy them? Of course you have. That's why you'll surely understand why I've done this to you. I love you and we belong together, forever. You understand, right? Of course you do.

Yours eternally,

Jimmy

The Superhero iii

38

'What are you fucking looking at?'
'Wha-what?'
'I said, what the fuck are you looking at?'
'Nothing. I - I wasn't — look-'
'You're asking for a slap you fucking arsehole'
'No. I was just - I was just-'
'I was just. I was just. What? Being an arsehole?'

The man at the bar with the potty mouth smashed his beer bottle on the bar, leaving a jagged, extremely pointy glass weapon in his hand, and waved it at a young man who had been enjoying a pint of cider. A little bit of wee came out of the terrified young man's winky, and his hands trembled, spilling cider.

Margaret had worked behind the bar of the Sailor's Arms for over 40 years and had seen her fair share of trouble. She saw the kerfuffle and knew she had to act — for Margaret was the superhero known only as: The Landlady.

Margaret ran out the back and down to the cellar. She left her superhero costume by the barrels. One of the barrels had leaked last Wednesday and now her costume smelled of stale Fosters. Margaret didn't care — time was of the essence and there was no time to spare — which meant the same thing, thought Margaret, who remembered the Fosters barrel needed changing and thought she might as well do it now whilst she was down here.

Margaret's powers were unusual and the stuff of legend. Punters would often tell tales of her exploits and reminisce over the times when The Landlady would keep the East End gangs in check. Even the Krays knew not to do business in the Sailor's Arms - not in Margaret's pub - no chance in hell. They feared her - and rightly so.

Margaret changed into her costume and made her way upstairs. Margaret was no more - out stepped *The Landlady!*

'Who dares bring trouble into my pub? The Landlady is not avin' it. Somebody's gonna pay!' said *The Landlady*, referring to herself in the third person like a twat.

Margaret you're too bloody late, again! said a regular, propping up the bar.

'Yer what?' Margaret was confused as hell.

'Yeah. That bloke with the bottle just jammed it into the poor lad's neck. He's bleeding out on the floor'

Margaret peered over the bar at the poor lad. He was indeed bleeding out all over the floor, gasping for breath.

'Oh bloody ell' said *The Landlady,* 'Nor again'.

The landlady's powers were the stuff of legend. But she was always late and hadn't saved anyone for a long, long time.

Rolos

39

Frankie tucked into his pack of Rolos with a great big smile on his face between mouthfuls. He liked Rolos a great deal, and wondered why he'd left it so many years since he'd had them.

He was almost half-way through the pack at this point and wanted to savour the experience, so he bit each Rolo in half, prolonging the scrumptious flavour of chocolate and caramel. He couldn't remember whether or not Rolos had a thin layer of biscuit within each bitesize chunk, but there must have been, otherwise he wouldn't have enjoyed the crunchy goodness he was tasting. 'Let's just check,' Frankie instructed himself.

Frankie bit half into the Rolo, and held it in front of him. He looked closely, squinting his eyes into focus, *What the fuck was this?* Frankie couldn't believe his eyes. Inside, tiny little iddy-biddy, incy wincy little pair of legs poked out of the caramel. It looked like a tiny person had made their way somehow into his rolo. How he'd managed to avoid slicing the little person in half with his guillotine-like incisors was a mystery. He felt nauseous and threw the chocolate sweet across the room! He ran to the sink and jammed his index and middle finger down his throat and threw up the last rolo he'd eaten. How many of these little fellows had he devoured? Holy shit — the crunchy goodness he'd enjoyed, must have been tiny person bones! He looked closely at the bottom of the ceramic basin and looked at a tiny little face. He wished he hadn't looked now. The tiny little pale face was looking straight back at him — except it wasn't looking at all — it just happened to be pointed in his direction. It was soulless — dead. In its final moments, the terrible fear in its eyes had been frozen in time. There wasn't much left attached to the head — but small spatters of blood, barely visible without leaning in and focusing, stained the basin around the head.

Frankie couldn't believe it. What was happening? Had each Rolo been the same? There was no such thing as little people, well, not this little, so was this all in his mind? There was no other way to be sure other than to check the remaining Rolos.

Frankie was scared of what he might find. Oh God, that crunch! Were the muscles and organs the key ingredients which gave the rolos their oddly satisfying flavour? He didn't remember them being this delicious in the past. *No, don't think like that — it's sick.*

He decided the best way to check the next Rolo would be to gently pull it apart, so as to not cause any harm to whoever was trapped inside.

He pressed gently into the Rolo, careful not to squash any surprise resident. The chocolate crumbled on the outside as he pressed down, and the caramel stretched apart like string as he separated the little sweet with his fingers — delicately, before the string could take no more and split in the middle causing two strings from each half to swing downwards — hanging like sticky ropes.

It was as he feared. Laying inside one half, covered in caramel, was the tiniest person; a little man. He must have drowned in the caramel, or fried in it when it was still bubbling-hot. Frankie took a seat on one of the stools at the kitchen table, slumped in despair, back hunched and holding his face in his hands as he stared at the table surface, horrified.

When he finally composed himself, he washed up the little man as best he could and placed him gently onto the kitchen table. He couldn't believe he'd been eating little people and not only that, he'd enjoyed them, every single sweet one of them. Sweet! Yes, they were sweet. And tasty, Delicious even. Mouth-wateringly so. He thought about how delicious they were and he salivated some more. *Oh it was so wrong!*

After sitting there for nearly an hour, Frankie looked over at the packet of Rolos. There were 4 left.

And then Frankie had a terrible thought.

Yes it was repulsive to think he'd been eating little humans - but not so repulsive that he stopped thinking dark thoughts about those scrumptious delights. He looked down at the little man, still sticky from caramel, and his heart sank. What a horrible way to meet ones end! What happened? Did these little people somehow find themselves in the rolo factory and somehow fall into a vat of caramel? Maybe he should call the factory and warn them? Maybe he could stop this tragedy from befalling more of them? But no, he'd sound like a crazy person, calling a chocolate factory and warning them about tiny people in their rolos. They'd maybe think it was a prank and some juvenile idiot was making reference to Umpa Lumpas in a chocolate factory. Nevertheless, it was too late for these unfortunate little folks and would it be so bad if he finished the pack? *'Oh God - what am I thinking!'*

A sudden sound made Frankie jump from his seat and stagger backwards. The little person had shot bolt upright and took the loudest gasp of air Frankie had ever heard — far louder than you would ever expect from a person the size of a pea — not that you'd expect a person the size of a pea in a million years.

The tiny person crawled backwards away from Frankie until he bumped into a coffee mug. The little man was terrified. 'What do you want? Please - don't hurt me!' Cried the little person.

'Calm yourself little man - I won't hurt you. I found you inside one of these little rolos and managed to get you out and clean off most of the caramel. What are you? How did you get into the rolo?' It was just as Frankie had guessed — tiny people existed — and in their search for a new home, they found themselves at the chocolate factory. They found the chocolate and caramel delicious and couldn't resist leaning in for a taste from the vat. It was only inevitable that an accident such as this would occur. Their greed had gotten the better of them all.
'My name's Sam' said the little person.
'Nice to meet you Sam. I'm Frankie'.
'Nice to meet you Frankie. Now that I've told you my story, I wonder if you could help me find my family? They may be trapped just as I was'.

Frankie felt sick to his stomach and a dread came over him, he knew he'd have to deliver devastating news. But maybe he could cushion the blow by first rescuing the others. Frankie reassured Sam that he'd help. And so he emptied the remaining Rolos onto the table top. Sam looked on, biting his nails. There were 4 Rolos left, lined up side by side.

'There are only 4 there! What about the others?' Sam cried.

Frankie had no choice but to lie, 'You were the only one - the others were just caramel - I checked - I always pull them apart before eating - it's like eating two Rolos that way'

'Oh thank God!' Sam's relief was palpable.

'I'll open the first one' said Frankie, softly.

'Please - be careful' pleaded Sam, 'My brothers and sisters could be in there. I have a son too'.

Frankie's heart sank. He may have already devoured them.

'This could be traumatic for you. Turn around - don't look. I'll check and if it's good news I'll tell you, if it's bad, you really won't want to see. I'll clean them up and rest them down for you to say your goodbyes. But it shouldn't come to that - they may be fine - back at the factory worrying about you being missing'. Frankie wanted to put Sam at ease, but dark thoughts began to surface and however hard Sam tried, he couldn't put them to the back of his mind.

'Turn around' Frankie asked softly.

'Ok, please, be careful' begged Sam, tears welling up in his eyes.

Sam turned and took a deep breath. Frankie took one too. Frankie picked up the first Rolo. He held it in front of his face and looked at it for a moment. *I can't. It's not right. But if there's another in there — it would surely be dead. Sam surviving is a miracle. But it could be his son! His brothers or sisters! No - I'll check and save as many as I can — or at least, give Sam the closure he deserves — good or bad.*

With that thought, and as if his brain had taken no notice of his conscience — as if they were two separate entities, Frankie popped the Rolo into his mouth, closed his eyes and chomped away, the juicy sweet flavours of flesh and meat beautifully complimented by the crunchy texture of bone, the chocolate and caramel enriching the special ingredient — the icing on the cake so to speak. Without thinking - Frankie gave a satisfying groan as he savoured the taste before opening his eyes and snapping back to reality. *Oh my God what have I done!*

'What did you find?' Sam cried, still looking away.

'Nothing' Frankie replied, guiltily.

'What was that groan?'

'Nothing. I'll taste - I mean, I'll *try* the next one. So far so good. SO GOOD!'. Frankie knew already that he had no intention of stopping, and he no longer cared — he no longer valued the lives of little people — because it didn't suit him — they were too delicious. *It's no different to eating chickens, or pigs.* Frankie didn't buy his own bullshit, but didn't care.

He seized the next Rolo and popped it into his mouth — this time chomping down on it and swallowing like he hadn't eaten in days. *Oh God that's amazing!* Frankie had to keep his mouth closed for a second whilst he swallowed a pool of saliva — his glands in overdrive.

'What about that one?' said Sam, his voice trembling.

'No, nothing Sam,' replied Frankie.

Frankie popped another Rolo quickly, worried that Sam was beginning to suspect something sinister. This time he bit the Rolo in half - red caramel slid down his thumb as he pulled away the chocolate from his mouth. Some red caramel had clung to his bottom lip and a fine string of it ran down his chin. The last Rolo needed savouring - he bit into it like the last - only this time, a scream came from within. Sam swung himself around and saw half a Rolo between Frankie's fingers. Frankie dropped the Rolo onto the table top, taken aback. 'Oh my God - what have you done!' cried Sam, who ran to the half eaten Rolo, frantically scraping out caramel from the chocolate shell - like digging a grave with his bare hands. He reached in and grabbed a torso and pulled. The legs were missing and the caramel ran red. The body writhed in pain. Sam scooped caramel from the body and wiped their face.

'Sammy Junior! No! God no! It's ok Sammy, Daddy's here. Daddy's here! Please - talk to me. Open your eyes! Sammy!'

Sammy Junior's eyes slowly opened and focussed. 'Daddy?'

'It's ok Sammy, Daddy's here!' Sam rested his head on his child's chest and sobbed. Sammy Junior placed his hands around his Dad's head and raised it, looking into his eyes. 'Don't cry, Daddy,' said Sammy, softly.

'Oh my Baby! My sweet baby! Sam turned his head to face Frankie, 'HOW COULD YOU?!'

Frankie didn't flinch.

'Daddy - what's happening? What's wro-'. Before Sammy junior could finish his sentence, in a split-second, Frankie had plucked up the boy and popped him into his salivating mouth and chomped away satisfyingly. Sam fell backwards and turned yet again to Frankie in horror. His eyes widened — shock seized him and he froze.

For a moment Sam sat still. Finally, he regained some sense of the moment. 'What did you do? You monster! You beast! How could you? No. No. Sammy!' Sam wailed, tears were now flowing like rapids. Frankie's conscience was desperately trying to reassert itself — and an ounce of it returned. Frankie looked at Sam with sympathy.

'I'm so sorry, Sam' I couldn't help myself.

'I'll kill you! I'll kill you!' cried Sam, propelling himself up and forward towards Frankie, who had retrieved the first Rolo he'd just remembered was still there in two halves. Frankie held half a rolo in each hand, and in a downward swoop towards the little man, the rolo halves slammed together, sandwiching poor Sam within. Muffled screams escaped Sam's chocolate coffin.

'I'm sorry Sam. I really am' Frankie whispered into the Rolo he held close to his lips.

'No! Please! No!' The muffled screams were now coherent words — faint but coherent.

Frankie savoured Sam. He seemed more delicious than the rest — perhaps more forbidden — more wrong and therefore more thrilling and satisfying.

Frankie wiped his mouth and chin.

I think I'll just pop to that corner shop again.

Flight F7401

40

Jasper had booked his flight to Kavos only last week. He was so excited to finally be getting away. He'd not had a holiday in over two years all because some gross idiot abroad had eaten a monkey brain soup starter, badger's anus for main, and sticky bat pudding for dessert; and as a result, a mutated virus caused a global pandemic. He may have gotten the details wrong but he couldn't be bothered to do any research into the matter. Specifics aren't important.

But all that pandemic shit was now over, and his holiday was all that mattered. Jasper had booked his flight online and it wasn't straight forward. The flight was dirt-cheap providing he didn't opt-in to any extras, like an onboard meal, drink, leg room, comfort of any kind, ear plugs, in-flight entertainment, oxygen masks and seatbelts, a life jacket, priority boarding, luggage allowance, or any sort of courtesy or respect from the attendants. Jasper wasn't having any of it. Fuck that. And as he saw it - flying was the safest way to travel and the odds of anything going wrong were so low, it wasn't worth a second thought. *Who needs a seatbelt on a plane?* If it crashes a seatbelt won't help - it'd probably go through your torso like a cheese-wire. And the discomfort? Well, the flight wasn't that long — he'd once sat through an entire episode of *The One Show* - so if he could manage that level of discomfort, he could handle limited leg room.

Jasper boarded the plane last, everyone else had seemingly paid for priority boarding, and as soon as he had got settled into his seat, he felt smug that he'd got on the plane only minutes later than everyone else without paying the extra twenty quid. He was however, very aware of the fact that the seat was uncomfortable and the fat man next to him was breathing louder than the engine. Jasper let slip a short, spontaneous laugh after thinking to himself, *'this plane crashing wouldn't be such a bad thing,'* and his impetuous laugh startled the annoying mouth breather next to him, who in turn made a point to express his annoyance with a glare.

The turbulence began about thirty minutes into the flight — and Jasper clutched both arm rests whilst his stomach tied itself up in a sickening cramp, and sweat droplets trickled from his temples to his cheeks. The turbulence intensified and the lights in the cabin flickered on and off as the passengers' arses bounced up and down on the cushioned seats. Sudden sharp screams followed every jerk of the plane and every sudden drop in altitude started with screams and ended in silence, as everybody closed their eyes and shared in the same silent prayer in their minds; *Please God, save us*. The flight attendants strapped themselves in to their seats. Jasper had experienced turbulence before, and never worried because he always looked at the flight attendants' expressions — if they were unbothered, or amused by the panic of the passengers, he knew it was normal turbulence and nothing to worry about — but in this instance, they looked like they were shitting themselves, and one flight attendant was rocking back and forth muttering the word 'shit' over and over again in quick succession. *Not a good sign,* thought Jasper. He noticed a few oxygen masks drop down in front of some of the passengers, who seized them and frantically attempted to strap them to their faces.

Obviously there's nothing like an oxygen mask dropping down in front of your big stupid face to save your stupid life when your burning plane hurtles to the ground at 700 mph until exploding into a fiery grave, to spice up your holiday. Who doesn't love an oxygen mask on a plane? I suppose it's supposed to make you feel safe - but all it did was add further panic - to those who had them, but especially to those who didn't. But let's face it, a stupid oxygen mask wasn't going to save anyone. And yes, I did say 'burning plane' - Jasper had looked out of the window and saw an engine in flames; black smoke bellowing into the air in a dark backward stream scarring the skies. The captain's trembling voice came over the speaker system, 'Everybody, this is your Captain speaking. We're encountering some turbulence and will be making an emergency landing shortly. There's nothing to worry about - oh shit - PULL UP - PULL UP!' The captain cleared his throat, 'as I was saying, there's nothing to wo-worry about, please stay calm and we'll get you on the ground as soon as possible'. Jasper let out the most inappropriate laugh again, much to the bafflement of the wide-eyed fat man. *Get us on the ground as soon as possible? Yeah but in how many pieces?* Jasper mused. *Getting to the ground as soon as possible was the easy bit. The falling from the sky on fire was already taking care of that.*

    The plane was now making a symphony of ear-churning loud noises that drowned out the screams of the passengers. There were creaks, bangs, cracks, rumblings, crashes, screeches, and explosions. A louder explosion came from the right side of the plane and the wing was tore clean off, taking a huge portion of the right side of the cabin with it. Passengers who hadn't managed to fasten their seatbelts in the panic, were sucked out of the plane into the air, and would spend the next minute or so plummeting to their impending doom in a state of drawn out terror and despair that torments the mind to contemplate. One passenger who hadn't fastened her seatbelt properly, was now holding on to her oxygen mask, attached to the rubber tubing, with both hands. It was the only thing keeping her from being sucked out of the plane and into a fucking nightmarish free-fall of a few thousand feet to the ground — where there was a very good chance she'd splat against the ground over a massive radius and end up looking like a dropped pizza on a patio. It was highly unlikely she'd survive such a fall. In fact, it's unheard of. Maybe Jasper should have purchased an oxygen mask? Maybe shortly, he'd be in the same predicament as the unhappy lady hanging on by a rubber tube over there. The tube snapped and she was sent hurtling backwards out of the cabin, with a look on her face that chilled Jasper's very soul. She was sent backwards into the plane's slipstream, not before slamming into a jagged edge of the remaining bit of cabin. Jasper let out another sharp audible laugh, *What a waste of money,* he thought.

The big man next to Jasper stared at him with an expression Jasper had never seen before, a horrified look merged with a baffled one. The man seemed scared of Jasper, who was no longer sweating or clutching the arm rests tightly - which seemed more disconcerting to the man than the plane tearing itself to pieces. Jasper was finding all sorts of things to amuse himself about this disastrous flight. 'All that leg room them lot over there have paid extra for and their legs have only ended up being sliced off by a flying sheet of metal,' chuckled Jasper to the man next door, further horrifying him. '*Now* they don't need the leg room! Ha!'

The wreckage of the plane was found thirty minutes after the crash. It was in pieces, and metal panels, plastic bits and bobs, luggage, people, and bits of people, were found scattered over a radius of fifty miles. The main wreckage had hit a field, killing a cow in the process. A single engine had landed on a bungalow on a lovely little suburban avenue, instantly killing Mrs Maureen Morris, who'd just made a cup of tea and had settled down for an episode of Bargain Hunt with a plate of digestives at the ready. Her little Yorkshire terrier didn't fair too well either.

News crews gathered almost as quickly as the emergency services.

'I'm here at the crash site of flight F7401 and I'm joined by the miraculous sole survivor, Jasper Cunningham. Jasper, what are your thoughts right now?'

'Well,' replied Jasper, *'I'm just glad I didn't pay for any of those optional extras. Waste of money. Just ask decapitated head lady over there by the cow'* said Jasper with a snigger, to the shock and horror of the news reporter and millions of viewers at home.

You know that dream

41

You know that dream where your teeth all fall out? It's quite common. It's true meaning has something to do with the fear of loss; of either something, or someone. Apparently dreams tend to communicate to us through metaphors — weird eh. So when Aisha stood in front of the mirror pulling out her upper central incisors, and moving onto her upper lateral incisors, and then her upper canines, one after another, before moving onto her lower teeth, she was pleased it was just a metaphor. Blood dripped, and then oozed into the white ceramic sink, painting it red. Aisha could taste the iron in her blood — it seemed so real. Now, Aisha stood looking into the mirror, her reflection smiling back a toothless smile. She wriggled her premolars and molars with her tongue. They were so wobbly — the kind of wobbly teeth that needed to be wobbled more and more — the temptation was irresistible. They came loose even more, until she reached into her own mouth and pulled her bottom right premolar from her gum, slowly, feeling its root sliding out from inside her jaw. It was a satisfying feeling, pulling out a tooth. And if you've ever had a wobbly tooth, the temptation to pull it out is impossible to resist. The same could be said for picking a scab, or squeezing a spot, or pulling out a rogue hair. Aisha had almost satisfied her insatiable urge to tug on her teeth until they slipped free from their fleshy slots. The blood still trickled down her face and neck like a twisted water feature. Her clothes were bloodied — in fact, she looked like she'd murdered someone in a most brutal fashion. But as I said, the urge was *almost* satisfied. She had her molars to go. And in she delved — one molar at a time. You might be forgiven for thinking the whole horror show was near an end — but you'd be wrong. You see, Aisha had a full set of teeth — she'd never had any extractions growing up — therefore Aisha had 12 more teeth to go. Out came the first and second molars on the bottom left, then the bottom right. Then upper-left. Then upper-right. She had 4 teeth remaining — her wisdom teeth — or third molars. These would be tricky, deeply embedded as they were, and so far back in the mouth that Aisha had to fight her own gag reflex. An hour of pulling, twisting, yanking and tugging passed by — and finally one of the little blighters came out. Blood gushed out — more blood than she'd expected — more blood than had come before. Aisha felt a little faint — but remembered this was just a metaphor within a dream. She wondered what loss she subconsciously feared — but then put such thoughts aside to focus on the task at hand. There were 3 molars left. Aisha felt the pain — but the satisfaction dampened it, as did the knowledge that this was all a dream; a very common dream. She wished she were having the flying dream instead, oh heck, she would have even taken the falling dream, or the going to work naked dream, over this one. But we don't get to choose our dreams — no more than we get to choose our genes. If we did get to choose our genes, Aisha wouldn't have selected the genes that caused her paranoid schizophrenia. But that was all under control now - she hadn't had any flare-ups or episodes for years - hence her coming off her meds.

Anyway, three more to go and then I'll wake up, thought Aisha.

Beard Theory

42

Once upon a time there was a man with a big grizzly beard, the kind that looked a bit dirty and might be the home of lice. The beard wasn't uniform in colour — bits of it were a kind of ginger, whilst other bits were white and grey. The ginger bits were closer to the old man's mouth — maybe it had been stained by food or nicotine, thought those who took the time to observe.

The man himself wasn't particularly interesting — perhaps that's why he grew the beard in the first place — but what was interesting, is what lied beneath that beard. Yes, it was easy to speculate about lice, but what really resided in that beard was far more fantastic and absurd, for in that beard, over many, many years, a self-contained Eco-system had evolved. It bustled with life. There was an abundance of life hidden away inside that wiry forest, from creepy crawlies (not crabs or lice), to purple microscopic wooly mammoths, to great reefs thriving in the microscopic oceans of his beard. The life in this fantastic new world was colourful and sublime, and in complete harmony. And just as our world has humans, the beard world had beard people.

Was this bearded man aware of the microscopic universe he'd unwittingly created and nurtured? Of course not. He was just a man. A very dull man with a beard. But the dull man was important, and the tiny beard-people that had evolved within his beard knew it. Just as we had learned about our universe and its wonders - the beard people learned of their universe - the beard universe; the beardiverse. To them, the beardiverse was vast and unknowable, at first. But as minutes passed by for us, centuries passed by for them, and their knowledge and wisdom grew. It was only a matter of time before they surpassed us in every possible way.

Long ago, the beard people's entire belief system emerged from the harvest - a world unifying event that came every five hundred beard years. At harvest time, the sky would rain food - so much food that the beard-people could stockpile it for centuries, ensuring their descendants would not starve waiting for the next harvest. A deity was imagined; one who cared for them and fed them. Places of worship appeared over time in the millions. Wars were waged between different groups of tiny beard-people, based on diverging and conflicting interpretations — which diverged and changed so much, that many religions were formed from the original. Purists believed the food harvest was a gift from God, but many started to believe God was punishing them — since a lot of the food landed on people, cruelly squashing them where they stood. The fighting was savage. Eventually wars became about land and resources — and the act of war had evolved too. The beard-people developed weapons of mass destruction and many perished. During these periods, the bearded man had quite an itchy beard, what with all the fighting and nuclear armageddon going on inside it. Time went by and the beard-people unified and collectively grew — becoming enlightened, and science replaced God. They first sent probes, then beard-dogs in rockets, then beard-monkeys, and eventually even beard-people themselves, into the skies above, in their search for answers into what was beyond the grizzly forest in the sky. They developed lasers, super telescopes, mass spectrometers, satellites, and quantum computers.

They developed teleportation devices, artificial intelligence, mind-data transferences, eternal life, holograms, and doors that opened on their own — they took a long time coming up with that one, granted.

Eventually their scientists proved their theory of the beard. They'd discovered they were beard-people — and it changed everything. Of course, they didn't call themselves beard-people — why would they? They'd only just realised at this stage, that they'd evolved within the beard of a giant bearded man who ate a lot — allowing them to feast on his beard-crumbs, which they now realised was really, really gross and they stopped eating that shit. The name they called themselves was Golumpofloops - don't ask why. The Golumpofloops came to realise that they were living on a being that would eventually kill them — whether it be by means of shaving, washing, or third-degree burns from some horrible house fire or arson attack. Plus they were getting sick of being crushed by those fucking crumbs.

So the time came when the Golumpofloops took action. They studied their beardiiverse for a millennia, and came to understand everything about it. They understood the biology and chemistry of the human upon whom they dwelled, and they used it to their advantage. In their desperate ambition to evade death and remove the hand of fate from their frail and precarious existence - they planned to eliminate the human - and their world. They reasoned that even in the human's death, they would have millennia to plan for a solution before the human's face and beard decomposed. They were on the brink of developing inter-beard space travel and some of their greatest scientists speculated that they were only a few hundred years away from actual inter-galactic space travel, as the Golumpofloops had explored far beyond the beard and the human-world - and were already more advanced. The Golumpofloops drilled deep into the dermal layers of their world's surface, and introduced nano-nano bots into the human's biological system. They were programmed to target what the Golumpofloops had deemed to be the human's most vital system - the central nervous system. The probes navigated their way to the bearded man's brain and enacted their final program - the self-destruct program.

And that's why people have aneurysms and die.
Worst DJ ever

43

'Welcome back listeners, the time is three o'clock, this is Out n' About Radio FM, and I'm DJ Dick Richardson. Today we've been talking about charity work. We had a call earlier about a charity collecting books for inmates. I mean, there are other charities I'd rather give money to - I'm not depriving little Timmy of his revolutionary leukaemia treatments by not funding cancer research, all because Barry the serial killer in Wormwood Scrubs wants to read Harry Potter. But what I am saying is, if you give to charity, maybe as a second contribution, if you have anything left to spare, you can give to books crooks.

Another tweet just came in from a Barry from Shepshed, which reads, *"Why do you always use the name Barry when you're describing certain groups of people you've often described as 'undesirables'? It's unfair and unnecessary"*. Well, thank you for tweeting Barry. I suppose it's just a really common name and the first that pops into my head when I think of the poor or criminal-class. I see on your profile that you look pretty poor, so maybe there's something in it. Haha only joking Barry - I love the poor. Some of my best friends are poor. Now for some Barry Manilow. Now there's a man who hasn't let his name hold him back - take note Barry from Shepshed. Here's Barry with *Copacabana*.

That was Barry Manilow - what a guy. More tweets are coming in - quite a lot of Barrys actually - but most of them I can't read out on radio, either because of foul language or because some of them are just outright unintelligible. That's the Barrys of the world for you. Barry Manilow would never use such foul language, and he certainly knows how to string a sentence together. Oh here's a lovely Tweet from Gary in Leicester. Gary says, *"Hi Dick, I was hoping you could give a shout-out to my daughter Danielle who's in hospital after a car crash that left her with multiple fractured vertebrae and a partially-severed spinal cord"*. Well Danielle - I too am no stranger to the horrors of lower back pain. So from one bad back sufferer to another - I wish you a speedy recovery. Although, not sure you should be taking up a hospital bed Danielle - but I'm sure there's more to the story than a bad back. Maybe your spleen exploded.

Now I have to make an on-air apology for some advice I gave last week that you've probably heard all about on the news. I won't be doing the agony uncle section of the show anymore - and I profoundly apologise for giving advice to a clearly at-risk teenager and not, as I should have done, is raise the alarm to ensure young Billy got the help he needed. You may know already, that Billy called into the advice section of the show and told me he was being bullied. My advice was benevolent and harmless, or so I thought. The advice I gave to Billy to deal with his bullies was to *"kill them with kindness"*. Unfortunately it was a bad line and the last bit was lost over the poor connection, meaning Billy only head the words, 'kill them' before the line went dead. I'd like to send my deepest sympathies to all those affected by the Bumbridge Hill High School shooting on Wednesday. My thoughts and prayers are with the victims and their families during this tragic time. Although some would argue that the bullies got what they deserved. But not me of course. And this one's for you Bumbridge Hill High School, it's 90s pop group STEPS with their cover version of the Bee Gees classic, *Tragedy*. Take it away.

Ok welcome back. Now that's almost all we have time for. I've had a lot of texts and tweets saying my last song choice wasn't appropriate. I'm sorry but that song choice couldn't have been more appropriate - I assure you a lot of thought went into that — and I personally wanted to play the Bee Gees version but my producer wanted to appeal to a younger crowd, even though your average Steps fan is probably now in their forties. Is that the young crowd you're talking about Suzan? You can't see Suzan folks, but she's in the studio behind a glass screen giving me evils. I've got another tweet from Gary in Leicester about his daughter — you'll remember she has a bad back. Gary says, "*My daughter has a partially severed spinal cord and may never walk again you fucking cretin — which is in no way comparable to your lower back pain*". Well, Gary, that kind of language really isn't suitable for radio, but the damage is done. And no your daughter won't walk again with that attitude! I suggest you concentrate on the positives rather than the negatives — *"partially severed"* you said. I'd take *"partially"* as a win if I were you Gary. Get well soon Danielle - you can do it. Here's a song just for you, it's Elton John with I*'m Still Standing*. If that doesn't inspire you then nothing will. Take care everyone - see you at the same time next week. Hold up, scrap that. My producer is whispering in my ear piece that I won't see you next week - this is my last show apparently. Well, fuck you Suzan. Take it away, Elton.'

You could never know what it's like
Your blood like winter freezes just like ice...

..And I'm still standin' after all this time
Picking up the pieces of my life without you on my mind
I'm still standin' - Yeah Yeah Yeah!

The Cremation of Charlie Hutchins

44

It had been a mild winter the year the Hutchins family moved to Brighton. David and Shirley Hutchins had only one child, Charlie, who'd turned 10 in August. He'd been spoilt rotten as David and Shirley felt guilty they were uprooting poor Charlie and taking him away from his school friends, which of course they were. They moved in January as they wanted one last special Christmas at their first family home.

It was now February and David had settled well into his new job at the hospital (his reason for moving to Brighton) and Shirley had an online business that was a success, her new location in Brighton made no difference, what with working from home.

It was a Saturday when the Hutchins family decided to go to the beach for a stroll. It was so mild for that time of year that nobody was dressed for winter — a stranger could be forgiven for thinking the Hutchins's were all modelling for a summer catalogue. David never really felt the cold anyway — so even in the coldest evenings, he would still only wear a short-sleeved shirt. Shirley would joke that David was born 'north of the wall' and so he was used to it. David would reply that being from Manchester didn't constitute 'north of the wall' and that A Game of Thrones wasn't real.

Charlie wasn't the type of 10 year old to constantly have his head stuck in a games console or an iPad or a television even. He had to always be active — running around playing football or climbing trees. It was hard to keep track of him but David and Shirley came to trust that Charlie was sensible enough to be trusted climbing trees and shouldn't hamper his development and sense of adventure.

'Daddy. Mummy. I want to go in the sea,' pleaded Charlie.

'It's too cold for the sea - just kick your ball around. Make a sandcastle or something' replied Shirley.

'But I want to go in the sea' replied Charlie, as if his mother's response hadn't really dealt with his initial request, which had now switched to a demand.

'Take your shoes and socks off - you can paddle and that's it. The tide will take you off out to sea if you go for a swim. And it's too cold!' said David, the pushover in the marriage.

'Yay! Thanks Daddy!' shouted Charlie, already closing in on the sea as he ran, waving back at his parents intermittently, his legs seemingly pulling him ahead rather than projecting him forward.

'AND ROLL YOUR TROUSERS UP!' David bellowed after him.

'You're too soft' said Shirley, rolling her eyes, shaking her head, then smiling.

'I know,' replied David, leaning in for a kiss from an obliging Shirley.

David and Shirley slowly strolled along the beach holding hands, occasionally glancing over to check on Charlie, who was splashing about and generally enjoying his own company. The slight wind had picked up and started to chill; even David and his northern biology struggled.

'Let's head back love - I'm bloody freezing' David admitted.

'Wow. Who are you? Where's my manly northern husband gone?'

'Very funny' David turned to the sea to look for Charlie. He wasn't anywhere to be seen.

'Charlie!' shouted David.

'Charlie!' shouted Shirley.

Nothing.

'Where's that bloody kid?' David said, unworried.

'Dave, it's not like he's climbed a tree, there's nowhere for him to disappear to. Where is he?' Shirley's change of tone hit David like a blow to the stomach, which now weighed like he'd swallowed a bowling ball. If she was worried, he should be too. David was no longer cold — in fact, his whole body became hot and clammy. He felt so sick and a lump in his throat stopped him from shouting again. He took a dry gulp as if swallowing a sharp pill, and tried again.

'CHARLIE!' His voice was panicked and broke before the second syllable. He tried again, this time even louder, running towards the water. 'CHARLIE! This isn't funny!'

Shirley ran even faster towards the water, way ahead of David. She called out his name over and over — more high pitched and borderline screaming. Other couples, dog walkers, and teenagers just hanging around, looked on, struck by a dread they never knew they could experience over a stranger. Some gasped, some put their hands in front of their mouths and some, after composing themselves, ran towards the water to help, and shouted Charlie's name along with his parents. Shirley cried aloud, only stopping to call Charlie's name again, before falling to her knees. Twenty minutes had passed since they'd last seen Charlie splashing around with a smile on his face,. By now, large curious crowds who'd seen the commotion had gathered on the beach joining in the search.

The life guard was called in, along with the police and an ambulance. An hour had now elapsed and the police had somehow managed the impossible and removed Shirley and David from the scene and took them home where they made an official statement and provided the police with a photograph and details of what

Charlie had been wearing that day. They couldn't rule out anything - including Charlie's disappearance having nothing to do with waves and currents.

Days passed. Then weeks. Then months. It was time to give up hope. Of course, they never did, but it was time for some sort of closure so they could continue with their lives, lives that had hitherto been dominated by grief and sorrow. A family liaison officer had suggested a funeral be held. It was highly likely that Charlie had been swept out to sea and his body may never be recovered, and he deserved a funeral just like anybody else. It was a strange suggestion they thought, but both parents decided it might be what they needed to move on — plus, Charlie was a great kid, much-loved by everyone who met him, and he deserved a proper final goodbye.

Shirley dived into the planning of the funeral head-first. She planned it meticulously, even going as far as to organise a cremation rather than just a service — which David didn't approve of, but thought he'd go along with whatever helped her move on. Shirley had decided the cremation would be of some of Charlie's belongings — a few toys, his football sticker books, and his Manchester United football kit. It wasn't until the day of the funeral that David discovered Shirley had placed the kit on a big toddler sized doll. Not as big as Charlie obviously, but big enough to dress in his football kit and look extremely creepy. It gave David the shivers when he saw the doll sporting his son's clothing and lying next to his toys. This was ludicrous — but too late to back out of. David just wanted to get it all over with now, and move on. *'Perhaps they could try again once some time has passed'* thought David, immediately scolding himself for having such thoughts at his son's funeral, even if it were a farce.

In the crematorium, family and friends lined up and took turns uncomfortably placing something of meaning or sentiment into the open casket of the creepy Charlie doll — which nobody commented on out of respect or disbelief. Finally, after everybody had said their goodbyes, David and Shirley stood over the casket and gently cried together. They held each other and whispered their goodbyes to their mock son. As they turned to walk to their seats, Shirley spun around and pushing herself away from her husband, shouted, 'Wait! I almost forgot!'. Shirley reached into her clutch purse and pulled out a bright blond hair clipping. It was her son's. She had saved it in a folder entitled, *'Baby's First,'* which was a collection of noteworthy baby firsts. There was baby's first haircut, baby's first bib, baby's first steps, baby's first words (written down in Shirley's beautiful handwriting she'd mastered on a £499 calligraphy course) and many others. Most were photographs of momentous occasions only a parent would care about, but some involved clippings, and saving things that really should never be saved - nail clippings being one disgusting example. David hoped 'baby's first cremation' wouldn't be added at any point - maybe a collection of ashes being morbidly saved for posterity. Shirley placed the hair clipping onto the doll, tucking it just under the collar of the Manchester United football shirt. David reached out after her and gently pulled her back and guided her to their seats.

The ceremony began. The vicar stepped forward and opened a hymn book, placed it on a stand, cleared his throat, and everybody stood up. The vicar had never gotten used to child funerals and it was the only time he got nervous and emotional. Weddings and funerals for adults became something of routine, but this he could never get used to. It would test his faith time and time again, but he always got through it and had to do so again today.

'Thank you all. On behalf of Shirley and David, I would like to express just how much it means to see so many loved ones here today for Charlie. He touched the lives of so many in such a short amount of time, and his absence will be deeply felt by all. But let us not forget, his absence is physical, not spiritual, and his memory and spirit will live on for eternity, both in heaven and in our hearts'.

The vicar's words felt meaningless to the grieving parents, but they nonetheless appreciated the kindness in them.

After two hymns, another prayer, and a biblical anecdote David had heard at another funeral years before, everybody was asked to be seated.

The vicar cleared his throat once more, 'And now, Charlie's father, David, will read a poem'.

David had been dreading this. He knew he'd struggle not to cry. He wasn't nervous as such — stage fright wasn't even remotely a concern, he was more nervous about losing control up there and failing to give Charlie a dignified farewell. He adjusted his tie, loosening its tight grip, and took a deep breath — advice he'd been given by the vicar himself when they spoke before the service. David took the Vicar's place, who humbly stood aside.

David had done himself proud. He'd paid a heartfelt tribute to his son and read a poem that he'd gotten from the internet after googling 'dead child funeral poem,' which felt so wrong, and David had felt the guilt even as he typed the words, but he couldn't write poetry, nor was his mind in any place for creativity. In retrospect, there wasn't really any need to type in the word 'dead' but that word in particular had played in his mind on loop since it happened — and David thought that by typing it out it would in some way expel it from his mind where it could no longer torture him. Even though he lacked the creativity for a poem of his own making, the words conveyed his feelings perfectly. After the poem, he added a few words of his own - all the words he wanted to say in paying tribute to his son. It wasn't difficult - he just let the words flood out along with his tears.

The vicar said a final prayer, and a conveyor belt slowly carried the casket towards some small closed curtains. Everybody knew what was behind those curtains - they knew what it signified. It meant finality by fire. It was a painful closure. The moment a casket disappears behind a curtain at a cremation, is often followed by wails and cries the like you'd hear on the news when the camera captures a distraught and horrified mother cradling the lifeless body of her child caught in an explosion from a terrorist-planted bomb. This cremation was different - the cries and wails were followed by high pitched screams - but they were not coming from the congregation, they were coming from behind the curtain. The screams filled the room and with them a feel of immeasurable suffering and agony. Everybody fell silent, looking ahead, then to each other in a confused terror. Then followed gasps, and groans, then words turned to screams and shouting - the loudest of which came from David and Shirley - who threw themselves forward and threw themselves forward onto the conveyor belt, which had now ceased moving. They clambered over each other whilst the vicar tried desperately to pull both of them back - a task requiring all the strength of God. The screams penetrated the souls of all — what was happening? Who was suffering? Who was screaming? Who was in so much pain? Was this a sick prank? There was nobody in that casket — just a doll. David and Shirley didn't ask those questions however, they recognised their boy — even his screams. He'd once stood on a jelly fish and the pain was excruciating - Charlie's screams were also excruciating for his parents — their pain worse than the stinging pain Charlie felt. But this was that multiplied by a thousand. Unlike a film or novel set in Victorian times when the fragile damsel in distress would faint and the stoic male antagonist would hold her, David fainted. Shirley continued her mission to claw her way past the curtain, fending off the vicar at the same time. Eventually, the vicar with the help of a few others who'd come forward, managed to pry her away and hold her, before she too collapsed. The screaming from behind the curtain had ceased. All but a few were evacuated. Some cared for David and Shirley, still on the floor, whilst the vicar and two others made their way through a back door which led to a side door that led to the remains of the casket and it's contents — of which there was very little — just ash, melted plastic, and black clumps of unknown cremated bits and bobs. An island of melted plastic within a sea of ash and soot-like remnants was all that was left. There would be absolutely nothing recognisable left if the furnace hadn't been switched off early by some poor traumatised employee pressing the emergency stop button. Nothing made sense.

Later that day, some of their closest friends and family sat down with the Hutchins's and attempted to console them. Deliberately, the family had volunteered David's cousin Simon, a scientist, to explain and rationalise what had happened. They knew his credibility was needed to explain the unexplainable, and the only chance at stopping insanity gripping Charlie's parents forever. Simon explained the pressure build up within the casket was so great, that the items inside, including the hollow, airtight doll, was sufficient enough to cause a high-pitched sound that mimicked screams, and the eventual cessation caused by the pressure levelling off. Simon didn't believe his own rationalisation, but wanted to, and hoped to God it was enough to help the Hutchins's get over such a traumatic experience. The family doctor arrived and provided sedation for the couple - who sorely needed sleep.

The only way Shirley and David could move on with some sanity intact, was to accept Simon's explanation - the alternative too traumatic and horrifying to contemplate.

A week passed. It was Sunday morning and David decided to follow his old Sunday routine in the belief it may help him function. He made breakfast for them both; scrambled egg on sourdough, with a glass of fresh orange juice and a pot of coffee. The newspapers were still being delivered as if nothing had happened — it felt strangely disrespectful that the postman and the paperboy still arrived everyday and posted letters and papers through their letterbox, but he knew it was irrational for him to think so since the paperboy and postman had no knowledge of their tragedy. And life itself doesn't stop to pay its respects — it goes on rather heartlessly — mockingly even. David opened the Sunday paper and tried to focus on each article. He'd read an entire page and flick over to the next before realising he hadn't taken in any of the words he'd read; they were just words. Until page seven. A small headline of a story that could easily be missed, seized David's attention — seized like a snake seizes a rodent — clamping it's fangs into the rodent's flesh and not letting go, then coiling its powerful muscular body around it's prey and squeezing. David was pulled in and squeezed painfully by horror and despair. He read the headline again, and again, tears rolling down his cheeks, before dropping the paper and staring vacantly ahead. The expression 'the lights were on but no one's at home' was most apt. David never recovered and nobody would ever be home again. Shirley hadn't read the paper and therefore would never know what the article had revealed, but she'd lost her husband that day, and took her own life a year later.

The article?

'Boy washed up on south coast with amnesia, in spontaneous human combustion mystery'

The article described the boy in great detail, his height, weight, estimated age, hair colour, and clothing, and was very specific regarding the date and time he'd washed up ashore, and the date and time he'd burst into flames in front of horrified care staff in the children's home. It wasn't the death of Charlie Hutchins that ended the lives of Shirley and David Hutchins, it was a short article in a newspaper.

Jurassic Show And Tell

45

Panos had brought his dinosaur collection into his school's monthly *'show and tell'* event. The classroom was full of children eagerly awaiting their turn to show off their proud possessions, fidgeting in their chairs in excitement.

Panos was second to last — by which point most of the children had lost interest in the class — being selfish and inconsiderate little shits by their very nature. But Panos was proud of his collection, and told his classmates all about how long it had taken to collect them all, and what each one was called and whether or not they ate meat or vegetation. He smashed some of them into others, making roaring noises and explaining, *'this one would eat this one — and this one would fight this one'*. The teacher, Mrs Leafhead, aware of the time and impending bell, thanked Panos for his lovely and insightful presentation, and ushered him back to his seat. Panos was satisfied that he'd done a good job and that his classmates envied his collection.

Pyotr was up last. Pyotr's Dad was a scientist specialising in cloning and genetic engineering. Pyotr popped outside the classroom, and returned all smug, with his real-life dinosaur. Panos was livid. Mrs Leafhead pissed her pants, quite literally.

Pyotr had brought in not just any dinosaur, but a Velociraptor - his favourite from the Jurassic Park films.

'This is Mr Bitey the dinosaur' Pyotr announced proudly. Mr Bitey was on a leash — more suited to a Yorkshire terrier than a carnivorous prehistoric predator.

Everybody sat motionless and Mrs Leafhead let out a frightful sound. The raptor decided to eat Mrs Leafhead, pouncing on her, snapping his leash in the process, embedding its claws in her chest, and feasting on her flesh. The children screamed and ran to the back of the classroom — wetting themselves on the way. Mr Bitey turned to the rest of the class, bits of Mrs Leafhead still dangling from his teeth and claws. He jumped up onto the teacher's desk, crushing half of Panos's dinosaur collection. He then lunged for the nearest child and devoured him quickly. Panos stared at his broken collection — his precious collection — and felt a rage take over him.

Panos lunged for the raptor and punched it furiously with all of his might — throwing one punch after another — inflicting blow after blow with his rage growing wilder by the second.

Mr Bitey was a bit taken aback by this. He became amused. Obviously Panos's attacks were futile. Mr Bitey shoved Panos away with a side swoop of his head, loomed over him, snarled to give Panos a sudden fright, and then smiled and said, 'You're alright kid - I like you'. He then left and headed home with Pyotr, only to return for next month's show and tell.

Cupid's Arrow

46

It was St Valentine's Day and love was in the air, as was Cupid.

It was Cupid's busiest day of the year of course, and he had much work to do.

Cupid walked down the high street firing loves arrow at everyone in sight — spreading love. Another arrow. And another arrow. 'One for you, my lovely. And one for you, my dear. And one for you, and one for you, and one for you doop-de-doo' he sang.

'Freeze! Drop the bow and drop the arrows! Get on your knees and place you hands on your head. DO IT NOW OR WE'LL OPEN FIRE!'

An army of police cars blocked the road ahead, and an armed response unit were lined up and taking aim at Cupid.

Cupid dropped his bow and arrows and slowly turned his head and twisted his shoulders enough to look behind him — no sudden movements that might startle the armed officers. The street was littered with bodies covered in blood, impaled by arrows.

'Oh shit — not again - I've had another episode haven't I?' Bob said to himself, getting onto his knees and placing his hands on top of his head.

Printed in Great Britain
by Amazon

da46e763-f0d5-49c7-8f69-690d20b5706cR01